Stone Cold Lover
By Mel Teshco

Stone Cold Lover
By Mel Teshco
Text copyright © 2015 Mel Teshco
All Rights Reserved

This is a work of fiction. Names, characters, places and incidents either are the product of the author's imagination or are used fictitiously, and any resemblance to actual persons, living or dead, business establishments, events or locales is entirely coincidental.

This ebook is licensed for your personal enjoyment only. This ebook may not be re-sold or given away to other people. If you would like to share this book with another person, please purchase an additional copy for each recipient. If you are reading this book and did not purchase it, or it was not purchased for your use only, then please purchase your own copy.

To my family for their never ending patience

Cover Art by Kellie Dennis at Book Cover by Design
www.bookcoverbydesign.co.uk[1]

---

1. http://www.bookcoverbydesign.co.uk

To my family for their never ending patience

Chapter One

Light make you still
   Dusk reawake
   To serve be your will
   The monster you must break

As the sun sank behind the horizon, Cray Diamond came to life with a start, the curse resounding in his mind as though it had been cast just minutes earlier, not almost a century before.

Breath hissed from his mouth as his muscles hardened, contracting in screaming protest. Then just as suddenly, they unlocked and released him from immobility.

He staggered, withholding a groan when circulation returned and the familiar pins and needles sensation stabbed through his body.

A flood of awareness hit his highly receptive gargoyle senses. With sight akin to an eagle, hearing better than any feline and the ability to register scent like a bloodhound, it took great effort to focus wholly within and commence his change.

Only many years of practice allowed him to quickly instigate the shift from winged flesh-and-blood monster to human, moving effortlessly through the transition without the pain he'd once endured in his fledgling years.

Loretta.

He jerked away from the darkening horizon where lights sprang to life like dazzling jewels along Sydney Harbour and its surroundings.

He had to find her, and quickly, before night became day. The curse had given him extrasensory ability, an instinctive internal radar to track down whomever he protected.

That his devotion to Loretta had somehow affected his psyche and scrambled his navigation was something he didn't want to think about right now. He had to get dressed right this minute, ensure he blended with the revelers on the city streets.

*

Vivid dreams wrestled with Loretta Shaw's consciousness, images that taunted her, reminded her of the mother she'd lost at so young an age. But, as though drifting from a dream and entering a nightmare, she became aware of the too-hard, unfamiliar bed and the man next to her, softly snoring.

She jolted awake and grimaced. What had she been thinking? She couldn't do this anymore. Couldn't pretend that being with just any hot male was what she wanted, what she enjoyed. What she needed.

No man could ever give her the affection and comfort of the mother she'd lost. And none could ever live up to the man she so desperately wanted.

Not anymore.

Amazing how quickly things could change. How swiftly pleasure became displeasure. Stretching like an overindulged cat, enjoying the pull and flex of sex-fatigued muscles, the warm, post-fucked, fuzzy feel was no longer enough. It never would be, without Cray.

She pressed a weary hand to her brow, glancing at the shadowed silhouette of the golden-haired stranger beside her. She blew out a breath. He looked nothing like Cray!

Last night it had been a relief to discover that Josh—John?—kept a fully stocked bar. She'd encouraged him to down yet another whiskey, another beer, until he'd have been lucky to perform even an off-note song. In the end, he'd only managed to lock his arms around her before he'd passed out on the bed.

Her nape suddenly prickled. Her pulse fluttered, her senses identifying Cray long before she flicked on the bedside lamp to throw light on the subject.

Clearly he'd found a way to break into the apartment and deactivate its alarm. But then, it was a talent he'd perfected these last few years.

"Go away," she mumbled, even as her eyes devoured all six feet five inches of him as he stood taut and moody at the end of the four-poster bed.

She shivered, less with unease and more with longing, though one could be forgiven for feeling the former. His black, military-style cropped hair and the scar running straight from the bridge of his nose to the hairline of his wide brow added to his sinister aura.

"Why, am I interrupting something?" His frosty, gray-blue eyes swept the scene and it was pure reflex when she touched her swollen mouth before curling a hand around her mussed hair. His eyes darkened. "Because from where I'm standing, your latest lover is out for the count."

She dropped her hand and sat up. The bedcovers tumbled to her waist, revealing the globes of her breasts, her nipples, which hardened under his gaze. "It was a big night." *And not in the way you think.* She managed a shrug. "He's recovering." She swung her legs to one side of the bed. Turning her back on him, she asked dryly, "Are you jealous?"

Feigning indifference to the simmering quiet, she rose and padded across the soft beige carpet. She stooped, retrieving her discarded clothes strewn in a trail from the bedroom door.

Cray would imagine the worst. Who wouldn't when it looked as if her clothes had been all but torn from her in a fit of passion? It might have started off that way, but ardor—at least on her behalf—had quickly dulled.

She wanted her gargoyle, or no man at all.

She felt the burn of his eyes scorch the air, spiking her nipples harder still. Her womb contracted as the whole of her body reacted to his predatory hunger. Yet even in her high state of arousal her mind whirred with a far different kind of longing as she awaited his reply.

Dear God, did nothing get under his skin?

She tugged on her black lace thong, chilled by his shot of mirthless laughter and then as quickly burning hot when he closed the distance with just a stride. She dragged in a breath when his arms encircled her from behind. His large hands cradled her aching, heavy breasts while his fingers skillfully stroked her sensitive nipples.

"Should I be jealous?" he asked.

Despite her best intentions, she reveled in his touch. She caught her breath as waves of sensation melted her against him like a long-lost piece of a puzzle. "You tell me."

Wry amusement overlaid a hardness she'd yet to crack as he said, "We could dance around a straight answer for hours but I don't have the luxury of time to play mind games."

His erection nudged the small of her back, indicating what game he'd really like time for if he'd just once forget his guardian role and relent to their attraction.

She wriggled, brushing against the impressive length of his cock and losing herself in his unyielding strength as she tucked her head beneath one of his arms.

"Don't you ever just let yourself go, enjoy the moment?" She hated the breathlessness in her voice, hated how he could be physically aroused but emotionally unaffected.

He stiffened. "Nice sentiments. But I'm never intimate with the one I protect. You know that."

She jerked free. Thrusting her head and arms through the floaty folds of her crimson designer dress, she pivoted to face him. "I never asked for your protection."

"No one ever does."

If she'd been anyone else, she'd have shrunk back from the latent coldness in his stare. But she wasn't anyone else and she'd known nothing but sacrifice from this man...this gargoyle.

Cray dropped into a crouch and grabbed her high-heeled shoes from beneath the bed. He motioned her over and this time she knew better than to argue. She'd pushed him far enough.

His hands cradled first one foot then the other as he slipped on her shoes. Diamonds winked along the straps crisscrossing her toes. Her eyes fluttered closed as flames licked from the soles of her feet and leapt straight to her already burning core.

"Such a thankless job." She cleared her throat and opened her eyes to his downturned head, almost giving in to the need to run her hands over his spiky hair. "Don't you ever wish for something in return?"

With one fluid motion, he stood, making Loretta glad she wore stilettos. At five-foot-three, she barely reached his chest but heels brought her eyes to his chin level. She tore her gaze away from his sexy lips and studied his unnerving face.

Stone cold really was an apt description for his unyielding expression. She should know. She'd tried for nearly three years now to bring his impervious emotions to heel.

A large hand snared the crook of her elbow before he escorted her toward the balcony's locked, sliding door. With a faint chink, it yielded to his force and slid open in a whisper of sound.

"I wish for many things," he growled, guiding her out onto the small platform nestled high atop the eighteen-story apartment block. "But wishes and dreams are wasted on a gargoyle."

I don't believe so.

She twisted to face him. Tilting back her head, she watched the intensity on his face as he blocked his human awareness and focused his highly developed, gargoyle senses. His nostrils flared as he scented the air, his large frame taut and still while he took in the sounds of the night.

With eyes that glowed feral and bright as ice chips, he swept the area, double-checking for insomniacs and early risers—for anyone who might potentially witness his change and their unconventional exit.

Apparently satisfied at their privacy, he shrugged off his black, ankle-length coat and draped it over her shoulders. She tugged the folds around her in a gesture of long practice, surreptitiously inhaling his brandy-and-spice scent.

And not for the first time was she aware of just how safe she felt, enfolded in his jacket, cocooned from all that was bad in the world.

Lights dotted the cityscape of Sydney, a faint awareness of dawn in the air when Cray shifted from human into a winged creature of the night and folded her into his arms.

The change was effortless. If Loretta hadn't known about his ability—his curse—she'd hardly have noticed the slight hunching of his shoulders, or the broadening of his body as bat-like, eight-foot-span wings sprouted from either side of his spine as he gripped her tightly. Only the wrench and give of his clothes, which fell to the floor in tattered wisps, betrayed his true shift of identity.

Shame it was dark, she'd have appreciated the sight of his masculine charms in the flesh. Even etched in stone, she'd not been disappointed.

Unlike the ugly and inanimate carved gargoyles that littered many gardens and lawns, Cray retained much of his human looks.

Oh, she knew he didn't see anything remotely handsome in his gargoyle form but he was so wrong. From the large and rather fine-boned sweep of his wings, to his more subtle physical modifications, he was fascinating.

The remnants of his shirt and pants fluttered over the balcony and she twined her fingers behind his neck when he climbed the railing and stretched his webbed wings with a barely audible swish.

Her heart thumped, her senses in overdrive as she went giddy with anticipation for the buzz to come.

Cray leapt high.

Chapter Two

Her belly dropped as adrenaline skyrocketed, the ground a blur of lights beneath them as the winter air whipped her long gold-brown hair into her eyes and bit into her skin.

He wrapped her close to his chest, pressing the coat fully closed to deflect the worst of the cold, and Loretta wondered what it would feel like to have him really care about her.

She fought back a sudden, weary sigh. He was honor-bound to ensure her well-being. She was his top priority, but only as her guardian, nothing else. Besides, if he did care, he would've retrieved her long before she fell into yet another stranger's bed.

Her grip tightened. She was a fool to wish he saw her as anything more than a spoiled heiress.

Clearly his low opinion of her meant little in the bigger scheme of things. No matter where she was, who she was with, Cray always found her and returned her home, safe and sound, if not a little more jaded and sex-weary after the novelty of intimacy had worn thin.

But each time it became a bit harder to conceal her true feelings, to hide her yearning to mean more to him than an inescapable burden.

The lights of the Sydney Harbour Bridge sparkled below. He dipped to the left, pulling his wings back in a rustle of shifting air as he prepared to land.

His skin was cool beneath her fingers. When the sun came up shortly, it'd become colder still. Stone hard and inanimate. The thought momentarily sucked away her breath.

Sometimes she wished her father had never discovered Cray was an immortal whose curse effectively made him a shape shifter. Human or gargoyle, Cray's sole duty was to protect a mortal. Without that knowledge, her father would never have pledged to keep Cray's identity a secret in exchange for his vow of guardianship over his wayward daughter.

And she'd never have known this man who alternately made her ache with yearning and burn with resentment.

Her heart fluttered. She'd forever abstain from sex rather than never see him again, never experience the wild emotions he aroused within her.

He glided low. A thick glass fence with views of the harbor materialized from the darkness where it rimmed part of a cliff face. They swept over the turquoise-colored heated pool lapping at the transparent barrier before Cray landed on the clipped lawn with a sharp snap of up-thrust wings.

Orange-red smeared the horizon and heralded the coming heat of the day. As he placed her on the grass, his hands lingered on her shoulders. "Leave me now," he said roughly.

Loretta stiffened. She'd never been much good at following orders, and quite frankly she was getting pissed at having to always slink away once his seek-and-retrieve mission successfully concluded.

She swiveled in his arms. Looking up, she examined his shadowed expression.

Oh.

Forbidding and fierce, yes, but he was also irrefutably aroused. And very, very naked.

She didn't need to glimpse his cock to know. The strain evident elsewhere, a reaction universal to all men—the glint in his stare, the warm flush just beneath the skin of his jutting cheekbones, the sheen of sweat prickling his wide brow—overwhelmed her senses.

Then, like a homing missile, her stare did drift downward over the broad width of his shoulders, the dusting of dark hair between his nipples that arrowed to a flat, washboard belly. *My, oh my.*

His smooth, satin-skinned cock stood proud and high, nearly bursting at the seams. Its head reared upward, sitting close to the indentation of his navel, his engorged balls sitting beneath like the heaviest of ripe fruit. Ready to taste.

Her lips parted, the tip of her tongue edging out to lick top and bottom. For a short while she'd managed to rein in her reckless, passionate nature in the hope that Cray would appreciate her newly found reserve. But where had that gotten her? Absolutely nowhere. In fact, his remoteness had catapulted her need for sexual fulfillment right off the charts.

With the softest of sighs she went up on tiptoe and linked her arms over his bare shoulders. Her fingers curled behind his nape, digging into the soft-textured bristles of his hair as her lips brushed against his. Nerve endings sizzled at the light friction, the taste of him, and she drew closer still, fully savoring his mouth, his passion.

He jerked away with a growled profanity and she stumbled back, one hand covering her mouth.

His skin might be cool to the touch but his mouth had breathed warm intimacy. She swallowed, tearing her gaze from his delectable lips that hinted at cherries and smoke, to his narrowed eyes, glowing hot in the semidarkness.

Bloody hell. If her timing hadn't been so pathetic, her long-cherished dream of being possessed by Cray would soon have become a reality.

"You must go."

She narrowed her eyes at his forceful command. She could just make out the tic of a muscle in his jaw as his hands curled into fists, his form silhouetted by the distant haze of approaching dawn.

Her eyes went wide. Of course! He didn't want her to see him change. But it was too late now. Much too late.

With a resigned sigh, he dipped his head toward her. Hands unclenching, he turned into the coming sunrise to face his fate.

Warm color sprayed the sky and quickly mushroomed out to touch and embrace everything in its path.

Cray raised his arms and crossed them at his wrists, his face twisting into a savage grimace—a gargoyle intimidation to ward off unwelcome visitors.

It was a stance he'd perfected. The many times she'd studied him in his statue form, his pose had never altered.

Mesmerized, Loretta watched as living, breathing tissue hardened into a rigid carving of stone.

She took a couple of steps forward, her heels sinking into the lawn as she faced him. "I know so little about you." She tilted her head to one side, studying the superb lines of his stone form. "I don't even know if you can hear me right now, if you can see me."

She ran a hand over the cold, muscular planes of his shoulders and upraised arms. A shiver chased goose bumps over her skin. "I have no idea if you can even feel me while I touch you," she whispered.

Her hand drifted low, to outline his cock. It must take superhuman—paranormal?—self-control to ensure every part of his body looked the same, night after night. He no longer had an erection but his cock was still impressive. She could only imagine—vividly—what his superb equipment would feel like inside her.

A current of heat hit dead center between her thighs. She closed her eyes with a ragged sigh, skimming a hand under the hem of her dress before sliding her fingers inside her panties. Parting the already slippery, wet folds of her vulva, she scraped a nail along her aching clit.

Her breath snagged, her lids flicked half-open. Her inert gargoyle was now a hazy silhouette. "See what you've reduced me to?" she said on a gasp, hot tingles firing along countless nerve endings and ricocheting through her body in ever-increasing waves.

She threw her head back, her fingers stroking in rhythmic circles. "I hope you can see me," she said hoarsely. "Because it would be killing you right now, wishing it was your touch making me come..." With a startled groan, she did exactly that, electric pulses making her quiver again and again.

She let out a ragged breath and pulled her hand free, allowing her dress to flutter back into place. "Whoa," she murmured weakly, stunned at the ferocity and suddenness of her self-gratification. But then, bringing herself to orgasm felt doubly pleasurable knowing Cray might be watching.

Her fingers glistened. She raised them slowly to her mouth, staring deliberately at his fierce, stone face as she inserted a forefinger into her mouth and sucked away its musky sweetness.

"I would much prefer to lick my juices off your cock," she said huskily.

"Loretta! There you are."

Passion instantly dissipated. Loretta dropped her hand and turned to face her father's right-hand man—her unofficial minder in daylight hours—as he approached. "Max."

He nodded his styled blond head but his warm brown eyes hardened upon seeing her swathed in a man's coat. His nostrils dilated as if he'd caught a whiff of her scent in the breeze. "I see you've been enjoying yourself again."

Her eyes narrowed at his surly tone. Yes, they'd had a week-long fling a few months ago but he'd known the score. With the exception of Cray, she just wasn't a one-man type of girl. As far as she was concerned, relationships were for the needy.

Besides, didn't he ever sleep? It was the early hours of the morning for heaven's sakes! "I had a good night." She raised her chin. If only Max knew it was really Cray's jacket she wore! "And he certainly didn't complain."

He'd been too drunk to know better.

Max stopped before her. *"He?"* An unpleasant smile curled the corners of his lips. "Tell me, do you even know his name?"

Her spine snapped tight. "Since when do I discuss my private life with the hired help?"

Damn. Where had those words come from? She'd never once felt more superior for being born into wealth—most times, quite the opposite. But it was too late to offer an apology now. Much too late if the grim look on Max's face was anything to go by.

"One day you'll discover the sting of rejection," he said through gritted teeth. "And I'll toast the gentleman who brings you to your knees."

Who said it would be a gentleman?

Her attention returned to the gargoyle as Max marched back through the double doors.

She swiped the pink-tipped nails of one hand through her hair. Perhaps she was a spoiled little rich girl who wanted the one thing she couldn't have. But she burned for Cray. And no amount of lovers could ever cool that flame.

She looked up into his carved face. "I'll be long gone by the time you come to life when the sun goes down tonight. I think the fresh mountain air is just what I need. If you can hear me, you know where I'll be." She reached up and ran a manicured hand along a granite-smooth cheek, her voice husky as she said, "And this time, I know you won't push me away."

Chapter Three

The veranda's sofa swing gently swayed as Loretta leaned back in her ankle-length, fleecy jacket, getting comfortable for the long wait. Tucking one leg beneath the other, she watched the growing dusk, and with it, an incoming gray-white band of rain.

Frogs croaked into song with the gentle patter on the tin roof. Within seconds, nothing could be heard but the din overhead as the sky unleashed its fury.

The tumultuous mood of Mother Nature seemed to echo her own and she welcomed the display—even when some two hours later the downpour still hadn't abated. She closed her eyes, drawing in a shuddering breath. *Please God, please let Cray notice me...want me.* Her lids flicked open and as she watched the rain she acknowledged the rules really had changed. The game plan was now on a whole new level.

Beneath her jacket, the ice-cold night puckered her flesh with goose bumps. A shiver slipped down her spine when the flash of headlights at last announced his arrival.

She'd put him at quite a disadvantage by coming here. The mountain retreat was too high for him to make use of the night air currents. Unlike most winged creatures, he couldn't fly. But he could soar through the heavens until his weight and lack of air thermals brought him back to ground.

This time he'd had to use conventional transportation to follow the "brat heiress who takes her safety for granted".

She shielded her eyes as the headlights arced over her, dazzling her vision. They caught hold of the tangle of trees that, on a clear day, framed the inland patchwork valley far below.

Cray braked the SUV in front of a railed safety fence and cut its lights.

Her belly twisted, warmth pulsing through her even as she rose, toed off her sheepskin boots and slipped out of her jacket before padding barefoot along the floorboards.

Rubbing her chilled arms, she flicked on the outside light and waited on the veranda's top step. And like an apparition, a fantasy brought to life, he stepped from the darkness into the circle of illumination.

He seemed barely conscious of the rain that stuck his long-sleeved shirt to his carved body like a second skin. His denim jeans plastered his muscled thighs, emphasizing the bulge of his maleness as he strode purposefully toward her.

He paused on the first step and looked up. The rain eased to mist as their gazes locked. His eyes glittered. "I can't give you what you want. I'm under oath to protect you."

Her lips compressed. Her hand clasped the rail beside her. "I don't want your protection."

I want you.

"Nevertheless, you need it. And I made a vow that if I had to guard someone, had to become close to them, it would never be on an intimate level."

Her throat went tight. It hurt. But it was his honor as a gargoyle that he protected, not her own. "And if I release you from that role?"

"Only your father can retract the oath."

"Then...I'll convince him."

He raised a dark brow, a half-smile pulling at his lips. "Even if Lincoln released me, the curse would compel me to find someone else to safeguard." At her horrified silence he added, "Besides, your dad is more worried than ever about your indiscretions."

She moved down a step, now eye-level with him. The light rain clung to her hair and moistened her skin, glazing droplets of silver over her sleeveless jade dress. Yet heat warmed her from the inside out, passion running lava hot in her blood and warding off the cold.

Head high, she forced a serene expression while unclipping the diamond studs holding the dress together at the front. "Better to have this one night than nothing at all," she whispered. Slipping the dress from her shoulders, she tossed it aside. She wore no underwear beneath. She'd planned her attack. The trick was all in the execution.

"You'll catch your death with cold," Cray murmured, even as his eyes flared. He stood stock-still, his shadowed expression doing little to conceal the tic of a muscle along his tight jaw. He'd seen her naked plenty of times and had resisted her even when hunger had scorched his gaze.

Not this time. Please, not this time.

She leaned forward, cradling his wet face with outspread hands. Her lips merged with his and she closed her eyes, savoring the taste of raindrops and masculinity, of barely restrained passion.

Yearning swelled as she sank against him, her bared breasts rasping against his sodden clothes. When bolts of pleasure shot straight to the throbbing ache at her core, before seemingly liquefying her bones, it was all she could do not to crumple in a heap at his feet.

His hands were suddenly on her waist, bracketing her in place with so very little effort. And even in his human form she was aware of his latent strength, was totally turned-on by the leashed power that wasn't just physical.

Could he taste her passion, her need, the burning for him that seared her soul?

Time seemed to slow and she held her breath. Then everything quickened to double-speed as he groaned and his set mouth softened and opened beneath hers.

Desire hit her like a shock wave, an electric current that sizzled the nerve endings along her lips and everywhere he touched. She gasped, opening her eyes and jerking back her head.

His veiled stare of frostbitten indifference was no more. His eyes glowed like a flame heated blue, snapping with fierce desire and longing.

Chapter Four

Cray sucked in a breath, slow and deep. He should get the hell away from her while he was still able. Instead, he drank her in as if he couldn't get enough, everything within him aching as it hadn't for almost a century. With her parted lips and rivulets of water cascading between her perfect breasts, he was reminded why the last three years had been a torture worse than being frozen in stone.

He'd held on to his honor by sheer force of will. But no longer.

It wasn't her naked perfection that undid him, but the stirring of wonder and need in her eyes. A wonder and need for him—the man.

Her desire had never been subtle. Except, this time was different. She'd let down her guard and shown real hunger. Not just for his body, but for him, the person inside. And the realization touched him far deeper than anything physical.

Scooping her into his arms, he growled, "You win." Long strides took them indoors, where he laid her down on a soft cream rug in front of a blazing hearth.

The minx really had gone all out to seduce him. Flames crackled and spat, throwing light and shadow on the log walls and caressing Loretta's slender form with yellow warmth.

He knelt beside her. She reached up, her eyes full of wonderment as she silently traced her fingertips along his brow, down his cheekbones and under his jaw, as if memorizing every line.

He sucked in a breath, forcing calm. Lord, she made him feel almost...beautiful. How tragic could he get! Loretta was sex on a stick and innocence all rolled into one, her beauty incandescent, the very antithesis to his twisted stone form.

Her hands fell as he bent low, pressing feather-light kisses to her smooth temple before moving down one side of her throat and sucking the tips of each of her exquisite breasts. She arched on a gasp and need seared through him like quicksilver as she pushed her taut, shell pink nipples closer still.

He swirled his tongue over the hard peaks of her rosebud nipples and her breath caught sharply as she writhed beneath his touch. He raised his head, swallowing back a possessive growl. God, if only he could reveal just how much she meant to him, how much more he wanted from her. How much he wished this *now* was for the rest of their lives.

His jaw clenched. He couldn't think beyond the present. It would be enough to make love to this woman who'd tantalized and teased him to the very edge of endurance. He'd give them this one night—make it enough.

He drifted one hand lower, over the satin-soft skin of her flat belly and past her dark gold, silky strip of fuzz. He parted her folds like a ripe peach, intimately exposing her to his stare.

Sweet heavens above.

Breath whooshed from his lungs. And when she moaned, her thighs falling apart, the last of his resolve blew apart as if it had never been.

Her beautiful pussy beckoned, and he gave in to his primal instincts and dipped his head with a hungry growl, flicking his tongue over her clit and around its hood, tasting her honey-musk essence. She whimpered, and when he tongued the open slit of her femininity with one long, hot stroke, her fingers found his scalp and dug deep.

His cock jerked, growing impossibly harder. Damn. He ached to grind inside her pussy with its sweet, welcoming juices. Ached to fill her like she'd never been filled before.

But first he wanted to pleasure her, wanted to hear her moan, watch her face as she fell apart, piece by piece, at every stroke of his hand, every lap of his tongue.

He inserted a finger and pushed deep into her wetness. She gasped, and then squirmed when he slid another finger inside and started a relentless rhythm. He licked her swollen clit, tasting her arousal and inhaling her delectable musk scent as a connoisseur would the finest bouquet.

He increased the tempo and pressure of his hand and tongue, relentless until the very moment he felt her inner muscles abruptly clench. She shrieked, coming hard and loud, her throat arching as she sucked in air.

Removing his fingers, he placed an outspread hand over the soft fuzz of her mound, holding her still as he sampled her essence.

Cream and honey. The dew rolling off a succulent plant. The first scoop of ice cream on a sunny and cloudless day. His lips twitched. He wasn't poetic. Ever. But she really did taste of all that and much, much more.

He lifted his head, his eyes feasting on her as she lay spread out for him like an all-you-can-eat buffet. *Bloody hell.* Food had never tasted this good, never looked so brazen or sensuous or inviting.

Fuck. He raked an outspread hand through his hair, forcing his eyes shut to the vision that had his cock in peril of immediate detonation.

He was no saint. But this long-simmering attraction would have tested the endurance of even the most trustworthy monk.

Truth be told, when each nightfall had seen his curse lift, it hadn't been his oath that had sent him tearing after the heiress to bring her safely home. A day spent imprisoned in his own body, dreaming and thinking of little else but Loretta—it drove a man to the brink.

She played with fire, risked her safety, flaunted it like no one else he knew. And until night fell, he could do little but wonder where she was, who she was with. Daylight robbed him of life. Only when darkness shrouded the horizon could he ensure she was safe.

His impenetrable cloak of hardness had been worn for so long now, it'd become part of him. Was him. Yet sometimes he had to wonder if Loretta guessed she was his Achilles' heel.

The thought left him lightheaded with hope and despair.

Aside from nighttime sex, he had nothing to offer a woman. The reality reinforced his need to remain cold and closed and distant. He could never reveal how much he truly did care for Loretta. How much he...

His eyes sprang open as Loretta stirred. She sat then laced her fingers behind his head, clearly impatient for his attention, for another taste as she tugged him back down with her. Her eyes held his, glinting with arousal. "Don't stop. Don't you dare stop!"

With a harsh groan, he capitulated. His lips branded hers. His tongue plunged inside her soft mouth, sharing her musky flavor as her body quivered beneath his like a live wire. Mouths still fused, he helped her strip off his jeans and underwear. She wrenched his shirt apart. Buttons rolled onto the floor, for a moment catching the light from the flames.

Her hands traced his biceps and the bared ridges of his chest. When she lightly brushed his nipples and they pricked to attention, he couldn't stifle a hoarse growl of appreciation.

One of her hands slipped low, her fingers so delicate and yet so sure as they enclosed his engorged cock, her hand immobile for a moment as she stared, clearly fascinated by his reaction.

He reared back and gritted his teeth, caught between the agony and ecstasy of near-release.

Only after her breathy, wondrous sigh as one fingertip discovered his bead of pre-cum and massaged its moisture over the head of his cock did he snare her wrist.

"Enough." The command came out like a whiplash—sharp and hoarse and biting. *Shit.* He didn't want this exquisite joining to be over before it'd even begun. He could be a gentle and considerate lover—later.

He kneeled and pulled her close before slipping her legs around his hips. A little of her delectable juices seeped, glazing his upper thighs before trickling like a caress over his ball sac.

His breath hissed between his teeth and his cock strained like an unruly mastiff on a leash. His head fell back and his hips surged forward, drove deep. Impaled her. He wasn't small and he felt the muscles of her tight pussy jerk around his cock.

Like an inferno unleashed, passion snapped and raged between them, an unstoppable force that was a reckless and uninhibited need to possess. To be possessed.

He released a jagged breath. When he rocked inside her, his strokes long and deep and fierce, she met his piercing stare with burning, half-closed eyes, met his rhythm, accepted every inch of his hard cock. Gloried in it.

The cherry-like points of her nipples grazed his chest, sending darts of pleasure straight to his groin. He groaned through gritted teeth, his balls tightening almost painfully.

Then her inner muscles abruptly convulsed around him. A hoarse cry tumbled from her lips a nanosecond before he surged hard inside her. He threw his head back, bellowing at the dizzying pleasure-pain spurts of release at last.

"Cray..." She went limp beneath him. Her crystal green eyes shimmered, bringing a lump to his throat. "Thank you," she whispered.

No. Thank you. He couldn't voice the words and didn't want her to read anything in his face that would give her hope of something he couldn't give.

He pulled free from the warmth of her body but was unable to mentally withdraw and leave just yet. He tugged her to him until her back rested against his front. His cock stirred, but for the moment he was able to ignore his physical demands.

He cradled her in his arms, watching with aching tenderness as she subsided against him before slowly giving in to sleep.

It took more effort than he wanted to admit to release her and dress. And still he didn't leave. He watched, at once protective and fascinated, while yearning for so very much more as she sighed with dreams, her breathing rhythmic and steady, her pulse fluttering at her throat.

He had no idea how long he stayed there, the fire snapping and hissing behind them, while he drank in the flawless line of her beauty.

At last he forced himself to move, to carry her into the single adjoining bedroom with its rustic furnishings and queen-size bed with blue-checkered quilt.

It felt so right, the way she snuggled in his arms like a warm, trusting kitten, the feeling of completeness—two parts of a whole that had finally come together after a long separation.

He called himself all kinds of a fool as he jerked back the bedcovers. His muscles constricted, steely hard, when he laid her on the mattress. He stepped back. He wouldn't join her. Wouldn't reveal to her just how considerate a lover he could be, after all.

Self-control. Discipline. It was his safeguard, his insurance against depravity.

It was hell to face the crack of dawn each morning and know in seconds he'd become inanimate stone while every one of his senses went rampant—a visceral high-octane rush without an outlet.

Much of his restraint had been lost from the moment Loretta had touched him in his stone form. His dick might not have grown in her hands, firm and hot and pulsing, but he'd felt the spark leap within—the warmth—as clearly as if he'd been fully functioning and...human.

Then when he'd watched Loretta bring herself to orgasm, it'd been like withholding a meaty bone from a starving, feral dog. He'd wanted her with a ferocity that had been ravenous, unquenchable. He'd wanted to fuck her senseless, to replace her hand with his mouth and have her screaming his name.

He'd wanted her as he'd never wanted anyone in his life. And that hadn't changed one bit. He may have taken the edge off his hunger for now but sampling her had only intensified the cravings.

He tucked the bedcovers high. A wry smile tugged at his lips. She'd bewitched him, made him forget for a little while who he was...what he was. *Oh hell.* His smile disappeared, a deep sadness engulfing his moment of joy.

He'd sworn to protect her. And there could be no excuse for breaking the oath he'd given Lincoln, her father. His identity as a gargoyle could no longer be guaranteed if he so easily dismissed the pledge which bound him.

If Lincoln revealed his secret to humans, none would idly sit back and allow him—a beast—to roam the moonlit streets or glide the velvet-dark skies. They'd sooner lock up his cursed gargoyle body than allow his freedom.

Besides, he fooled himself if for one moment he believed Loretta could love the stone gargoyle he became at daylight, or the twisted, disfigured monster any other time he wished, as much as the human form she fancied.

She deserved better.

Their night of passion would not be repeated.

Chapter Five

For the first time in too many days to count, Loretta woke alone. She didn't care. She was satisfied. Fulfilled. Replete.

She was happy.

She grinned and then winced as she rolled over. She'd been with countless men over the years with little or no memory of the event. What she'd experienced with Cray had been unforgettable and had gone way beyond an extraordinary lay.

Oh, he'd filled her to the very limits and had had her bucking and writhing beneath him. But it'd been so much more than that and now her aches were a physical reminder of the most emotional, joyful experience of her life.

With a little sigh, she sat up, rubbing sleepy eyes as the late morning warmth caressed her face through the open wooden slats on the window. The pungent scent of eucalyptus drifted in, the air crisp and mountain fresh.

She peered at the bedside clock. In a couple of hours it would be midday. She'd never slept half the morning away before. Then again, her body had never hummed with such lethargic bliss, never felt so thoroughly fucked and sated.

She smiled sleepily. She could get used to this. Used to finding pleasure in the darkness with Cray, then sleeping in daylight hours as most other humans went about their lives, completely unaware.

She kicked the bedcovers aside and climbed out of bed, the floorboards warm underfoot.

Cray would be stone now. But where was he? Delight dissipated. Her teeth gnawed the edge of her bottom lip. In the past he'd always managed to get her back to her father's house before sunrise. He'd always ensured she was close by before he became an inanimate gargoyle.

She raced outside barefoot and bare-assed, wondering inanely how many birds, wallabies and koalas would appreciate the view.

She stilled on the veranda, her belly twisting into a tangle of knots. Beside the fierce gargoyle who safeguarded the steps leading to the veranda and front door stood Max.

Her gaze flew to the other four-wheel-drive vehicle that was parked beside Cray's. No way. A slow burn filled her until she wondered if her skin might steam. Her father had obviously told Max about this mountain retreat!

Max didn't acknowledge her presence. Instead, he stabbed a finger toward the gargoyle and snarled, "What is that thing doing here?"

Her vision narrowed. Damnation. Aside from her father, not one person had ever imagined that Cray, the bodyguard, was also Cray, the gargoyle.

Would he spot the similarities and make the connection? She had to distract him, and quick.

She swiped up the wet dress she'd left on the steps the night before and pressed it against her like a shield. "Good morning to you too, Max."

He swiveled around. His eyes widened and then burned hot as he looked her slowly up and down. "You're not dress—"

"Yes, I know." She scraped a hand through the wild tangle of her long hair even as she fought a tide of revulsion. What had she ever seen in him? Or perhaps every man would now fall short beside Cray. She forced a smile. "It's nothing you haven't seen before."

He shoved away from the lifeless Cray. His change in body language was dramatic as he fisted his hands, the veins on his neck and forehead popping. "Do you have any idea what seeing you like...like *that* does to me?"

She glowered. Fine! She dragged the still-wet folds of the dress over her head and snapped it into place. "Better?"

Ramrod straight, his eyes overly bright and his face mottled as if he'd glugged a bottle of poison, he rasped, "Better? No! In fact, things have been sliding downhill from the moment our relationship ended."

"Relationship?" she squeaked, disbelief burning her face. "I never once led you to believe there could be anything more than—"

"What?" he snarled. "A week of unbelievable pleasure, a taste of what I craved for a lifetime." He didn't wait for a reply. His hard stare swept the area, clearly seeking further evidence of her apparent crime. "Where's your lover? Who is it this time?"

Her teeth clenched. "That's none of your business."

The air vibrated with tension as he choked out a brittle laugh. "Let me guess—you don't know *his* name, either?"

His contempt scraped her nerves dry. "You needn't worry. I've known him for the longest time." And had wanted him from the start.

Hostility darkened his expression and he lunged toward her. His hand curled like a vise around her arm and her breath hissed from the pain that speared all the way to her fingertips.

His face contorted with rage, bitterness lacing his voice. "He must have been good. You couldn't even wait to get inside before getting your gear off."

A chill shot down her spine. *Dear Lord, no.* She'd known deep down that he wasn't a gentleman, but this? He'd become an unrecognizable stranger.

She struggled against his hold but his fingers bit harder into the soft flesh of her upper arm. "Let me go, you bastard."

He hauled her down the steps. She stumbled, gasping alarm as he jerked her upright, past the gargoyle and toward his vehicle.

"Oh, I don't think so," he said, his voice now eerily calm.

Shit. She cast a frantic look over her shoulder to where her guardian remained immobile. Cray couldn't assist her now. And she couldn't help but wonder if the farther this lunatic took her, the less likely he'd be able to track her down.

"You'll never get away with this." But her avowal was undermined by the high-pitched quaver stealing her voice. "Where do you think you're taking me?"

Ignoring her, he manhandled her along the dirt driveway toward his SUV.

Why hadn't she listened to Cray's repeated warnings? The gargoyle's face blurred, tears of shame mingling with fear as Max thrust open the door and pushed her into the vehicle with more strength than she knew he possessed.

He snapped the seat belt across her torso and between her breasts, the wet dress almost transparent. When it clicked into place, she felt like some helpless, disobedient child. He straightened and she flinched as he lifted a hand to tuck a strand of hair behind her ear.

"Escape is futile." He cocked his head to the side. "I'm taking care of you now."

Over my dead body.

She shivered and something told her not to give in to the urge to make a run for it. If he caught her, she really would pay with her life. Of that, she was utterly certain.

She didn't respond. Not yet. She had no doubt he'd gone right over the edge. But she wasn't about to simply fade into the background. She'd never been some shy, retiring wallflower and Max understood that more than most.

She waited until he climbed into the driver's seat and turned the ignition. "Look, if it's money you want, my dad—"

He cut her off with an upraised hand. "Don't dare debase what I feel," he said disgustedly. Reversing with a spin of tires, he then ground the stick into first gear and sent them hurtling forward.

She twisted around in her seat, watching numbly while her gargoyle became a distant speck then disappeared altogether as the car took a corner.

She turned to the front. *Oh God.* Would Cray try to follow and rescue her out of a sense of duty, or would it be something personal this time?

Let it be the latter. Please God, let it be the latter.

Max turned to her with a look of cold amusement. "You were always mine," he said. "I've waited so patiently for you, even while you defiled yourself, sullied yourself, became a slut."

He dragged in a breath and let it out slowly, his soulless eyes raising the hairs on the back of her arms.

"I gave you a chance, my love, but even I can only take so much. This time you've pushed me too far. The only way I can help you now is to set you free."

He looked ahead as he changed gears, a glacial cruelty revealed in every line of his profile. The vehicle lurched along the potholed road. Ahead she could see the ground on one side of the road give way to empty air.

"Max, slow down." *Please.*

His lips thinned into a hard white line. "I'm no longer your employee." His eyes sparked with menace and the engine whined as he pushed it even harder.

Icy dread crept through her, momentarily stealing her breath and making her shiver.

He threw her an annoyed look. With a disgusted snort, he motioned toward the backseat. "There's a jacket in the back. Cover yourself before you catch your death with cold."

Yes, I should be cozy and healthy when you kill me.

She forced her uncooperative limbs to move. Perversely, her mind worked furiously as she noted the embankments on either side of the road. She reached over and grabbed the fleecy overcoat which was laden with his cloying scent of mint aftershave.

She swallowed back the bile rising in her throat. This was her chance to increase the odds of survival to better than nil.

Bunching the jacket in her fist, she hurled it at his head. He grabbed at it, and she seized the steering wheel, jerking it toward the rocky hillside strewn with stunted gum trees.

Max jammed his foot onto the brake pedal. Wrestling back the steering wheel, he slammed the car back onto the road, stones spraying from its wheels.

He spun to face her. Adrenaline had clearly unhinged him further, his face manic with rage. Eyes shooting fanatical wrath, he swung back an arm and raised a bunched fist. "You crazy bitch!"

Chapter Six

Cray scanned the valley far below, his gargoyle vision detecting every shift and nuance of movement below as thoughts consumed him.

For so long he'd been an outcast. Ever since the curse he'd been unwanted. An intruder.

Only with Loretta did he feel differently. She didn't hide her passion and feelings behind a coy smile and shy come-on looks. She was genuine. And so very precious.

He'd been young, foolish, arrogant and still human when he'd given in to his desire for the beautiful and very married Elizabeth Ardell. She'd lusted after him every bit as much as he had her. Until her husband had discovered them in bed.

Perhaps if he'd believed the dark whispers concerning Elizabeth's husband, he'd have thought twice before sating his lust. But he'd never believed in mage craft, particularly that which was said to rival Merlin's.

It had been a hard lesson to learn.

His daily entombment in stone had given him plenty of time to rue the day he'd yielded to the temptation of Elizabeth's peachy mouth and sultry bedroom eyes.

All his hopes and dreams for his life would never become a reality. And a family, children? Never. In his human form he'd shot his seed into enough women to know he couldn't reproduce. Perhaps it was a good thing. His gargoyle DNA wouldn't be passed along to another victim of his own making.

Loretta...I'm so sorry. I can't ever give you what you want.

Faraway branches swayed, leaves shivering in the twilight breeze. A colony of gray-headed flying foxes winged through the air, searching for nectar, pollen and fruit.

He paid little heed. His focus centered on one thing—Loretta.

He breathed in, long and deep. *Thank God.* He'd caught a drift of her scent, vague and abstract, but nevertheless within radius of his gargoyle senses. He needn't rely solely on his radar instincts. Max had a huge head start and Cray's internal antennae told him the madman wasn't taking Loretta back to the city. He was heading even farther into the mountains.

He'd felt helpless, impotent, when he'd watched Max kidnap Loretta. Fury and fear like none before had burned within and grown with every passing minute of his frozen imprisonment.

Damn his inability to move and his curse with its weight of obligations that seemed heavier with each passing day.

Somehow he contained the burning rage, forced a deep calm the moment he unlocked from stone. His rationale would not be compromised, not at the expense of Loretta's life. Even so, his pulse lurched at the constraint. Some undeniable sixth sense prickled his senses.

Time was of the essence.

He unfurled his wings. Stretching them wide, he leapt from the post and rail security fence and into the sheer drop on its other side. An updraft snatched him skyward. He wheeled to the right and dropped his wings to counterbalance, soaring high.

Stars whitewashed the horizon, the air fresh, crisp and unpolluted by the smog of the city, some three hours' drive east.

From this vantage point, the road's descent cut through the green foliage like a rust-colored vein. Wattle and huge gum trees at times yielded on one side to a jagged cliff face.

Twice, his weight and thinning air currents forced him to ground. Scrambling and climbing his way back up the nearest summit, he dove off its cliff face, once again able to soar through the sky and steadily gain on his prey.

A tightness in his belly receded as he pinpointed a faraway, thinning plume of dust. Airborne, it would take just minutes for him to catch them.

He smiled when he spied them far ahead, where Max's SUV hurtled down the twisting, steep road.

Headfirst, arms back and wings tucked by his sides, he dropped from the sky like a stone missile. Wind whistled past, disabling any ability to scent, to hear breath or heartbeat—to know if Loretta was safe and sound—alive or, God forbid, dead.

With a sudden shift of motion, he snapped his wings out and lifted them back. The force jerked him upright, and pivoted his legs beneath him just a millisecond before he landed on the hood of the moving car.

Chapter Seven

Blood trickled from Loretta's nose. One eye was puffed closed and throbbed like hell, but suddenly she didn't much care.

Cray had found her.

She peered through her good eye and watched in awe as Cray settled onto the front of the SUV. Max shrieked in horror, curses tumbling from his mouth.

With wings outstretched for balance, Cray looked like some glorious, avenging angel. He looked up. When he saw her bloodied face his head jerked back. His stare narrowed, and then turned crystalline cold.

Her throat dried, and Max stared at the gargoyle with wild, disbelieving eyes. With another round of curses, Max swerved the vehicle left and right, but Cray didn't budge. "Tell me that thing isn't real."

"No can do." She swiped blood from her face. "Say hello to my guardian, Cray Diamond."

He gaped, his gaze glued to the gargoyle on the hood who had murder in his eyes. His breath wheezed. "Cray?"

"Yes." She grabbed the jacket from where it'd tumbled onto the floor. Unsnapping her seat belt, she thrust her arms into the jacket's sleeves and pulled its edges tight around her, then clipped her seat belt back on. She turned to Max. "The one and same you've met at countless dinner parties." And felt intimidated by.

"Oh dear god." Max rubbed a shaky hand over his sickly green face. He shot her a look of disgust. "It's him, isn't it? He's the one you fucked at the cabin."

He made it sound so dirty, so vile. How could he get it so wrong? She raised her chin while she watched Cray inch forward in the peripheral vision of her good eye. "Yes."

Max curled a lip and shook his head. "How could you sink so low?"

"That's rich, coming from a man who hits women." She took a steadying breath as his mouth tightened defensively. She didn't need to hear his excuses. "Being with Cray..." she paused, her voice softening as she recalled their intimacy. "It was the most beautiful experience of my life."

Something between a howl and a snarl burst from Max's compressed mouth, followed as suddenly by a wild laugh. "Isn't that sweet? I just hope you enjoy taking that memory with you to your grave!"

He jammed his foot on the accelerator and spun the steering wheel toward the cliff face. The vehicle skidded sideways and bounced across ruts, before pitching, smooth as silk, through the air.

She cried out, but no words sounded. Breath hitched in her throat as Cray surged forward on the tilting hood, the heel of his hand shattering the windshield.

Time seemed to slow as she flicked Max a look. Why had he done this? What had happened to the man she thought she knew? Impossible to believe they'd both die like this.

She turned back to Cray. God, regrets, so many of them, flashed through her head in that instant. She couldn't lose him. Not now.

The vehicle careened into some part of the hard cliff face. Breath whooshed from deep in her chest. Her left shoulder slammed against the doorframe and she let out an agonized cry before her head struck the side window with a sharp crack.

She closed her eyes against a flood of scalding tears. Metal crunched, more glass shattered, and then silence. Her eyes flew open. Out the side window, the world righted itself as the SUV again arced through the air.

This was it, then.

Her eyes caught and held Cray's. *I love you.*

His stare widened and glittered bright and sharp as diamonds scattered beneath the sun.

Max took hold of her hand and gave an apologetic squeeze. His fingers slipped away as Cray unbuckled her and grasped her upper arms.

Cray's muscles bunched and flexed as he lifted her close. She gripped his shoulders and he abruptly vaulted through the broken windshield. A vacuum of air greedily sucked, then his wings snapped out and halted their free-fall and they drifted gently on the breeze.

A heavy thud sounded, followed by an awful screech of metal. A bright flash lit up the night sky as a sharp explosion shook the ground and impacted the updraft that carried them.

Cray tucked her head under his chin, shielding her from the acrid smoke. His lips brushed her hair, and he said gently, "Close your eyes."

Chapter Eight

Cray felt a twinge of sadness as he watched the flames twist and warp the blackened metal below. The emotion dissipated quickly when Loretta moaned and moved weakly in his arms, her profile revealing her bruised and bloodied face.

Anger rose inside him. That the bastard had dared lay a hand on her was almost beyond his comprehension.

"It's okay, sweetheart." They were descending fast, but amongst the treetops in the distance he could see the old tin roof of a farmhouse. "No one will ever hurt you again." *I'll make sure of that.*

He dropped to the ground and immediately shifted into human form.

Minutes later, an elderly woman with her gray hair pulled back into a tight bun, opened the sagging front door and peered through the screen door.

Cray swallowed an impatient urge to push his way inside. "We need help."

Alarm radiated from the woman like something tangible and she put a mottled hand to her mouth, suppressing a gasp.

Her reaction was understandable. He was stark naked and Loretta lay bloodied, bruised and trembling in his arms. "Please," he said. Loretta looked deathly pale and it took all his willpower to wait outside.

The lady hovered uncertainly at the doorway, relenting only after glancing once more at Loretta's ashen face. She stepped aside and peeled open the door before motioning him in. "Of course."

He stepped through the door and she swept an arm toward an outdated couch. A frayed, crocheted blanket did little to hide its condition. "Put her there. I'll ring for an ambulance." Brisk now, she marched into another room. A moment later, he heard the muted, no-nonsense tone of her voice through the open door.

His focus stayed with Loretta. God, she was pale. At least her breathing had steadied. Pushing some hair off her blood-crusted brow, he murmured, "You'll be taken care of now. I wish I could stay but the medics will be here soon." With dawn on their heels.

"You're going?" asked the gray-haired lady.

He jerked his attention to her. She stood straight-backed and clearly scandalized beside the door. He mentally cursed his second-rate human senses. He should've focused his gargoyle abilities—the elderly lady was as spry as a cat!

He rubbed a hand over his face. "I have no choice." Hell, to admit it was like tearing out a piece of his heart.

"Young man, we all have choices," she said primly. Her eyes didn't stray below his neck as she approached. Her floral scent tickled his nose and masked the aged, moldy odor permeating the house. "The trick is making the right one."

He stood, well aware that he towered above the old lady, dwarfing her. Add the fact that he was naked and he almost smiled at her tenacity in giving him a lecture. "I only wish you were right."

With one lingering look at Loretta, he headed for the door. He didn't look back when he pushed it partway open and added, "Thank you for your hospitality." He would ensure the little old lady was rewarded well for her help.

With that, he strode outside, cursing the hex that now forced him to leave Loretta alone when she needed him most.

Chapter Nine

Loretta shivered as she watched her father pay his respects at Max's graveside. Stooped and trembling in a wheelchair, he seemed so very much older than ever before.

The smell of freshly dug earth brought back haunting memories and she swallowed back a sob. This was all her fault. No one was safe to love her...to protect her. Her selfish core tainted anyone who did.

"Retta. Let's go home."

She started at her father's torn voice, at his feeble touch. His ropy-veined hand looked frail on hers, his upturned face was grief stricken and...broken.

"Yes." She hadn't realized the funeral had concluded, and the mourners were now all heading back to their cars.

It was still hours until dark. The unseasonably hot, midafternoon sun beat with relentless force on her bare shoulders with just the spaghetti straps of her black dress for protection.

She desperately needed to feel Cray's arms around her, hear his soothing voice. Only, since the accident and their one night of passion, he'd distanced himself from her both physically and emotionally.

It was as if his human form was the one carved from stone. Didn't he know how much she needed him now, how much she missed him?

She watched as the gravediggers threw soil onto Max's coffin.

Despite the heat, a rash of goose bumps spread over her arms. She might never understand Cray's indifference but at least he was safe. Alive.

A tear slipped down her face. On heavy limbs she turned, following her dad's burly nurse as he pushed the wheelchair back to the waiting car.

*

The last few evenings Cray had found a savage kind of comfort in the agony of returning circulation and unlocking muscles. If physical pain helped him forget the constant ache deep in his chest, even just for a moment, then he'd welcome it anytime.

But no amount of painful reawakening could dim the gut-wrenching misery as he watched, frozen in stone and outwardly silent, while Loretta paced before him. Her stress and grief were etched into every fragile bone of her face. Her joy sucked right out of her.

"Cray!" Relief filled her voice when she realized he'd come to life. Elation sparked in return but was quickly snuffed. *Fool.* He didn't expect Loretta—any woman—to become attached to a man who was a slave to a string of words chanted almost a century ago.

Bad enough that he was stone much of the time but to one day be forced away from her while guarding someone else, perhaps half a world away...

He inwardly shuddered then stiffened as she threw her arms around him. God, what he wouldn't do to return her embrace. Her curves pressed against his nakedness felt so right—too right, according to his body's instant reaction.

She smelled divine—subtle notes of vanilla and frangipani. He took another breath and forced himself to step back, his wings snapping closed behind him. "You shouldn't be here right now."

Her thick-lashed eyes dropped, her pretty-as-a-pansy mouth drawing tight. "Don't worry. You're safe. No one followed, no one saw you come alive."

Damnation. She'd been through hell and back, and he worried about preserving his identity! He moved back to her and tugged her close, wrapping his arms around her as he indulged in the simple intimacy. "Of course no one followed you. And I'm glad you're here."

"Thank you," she whispered, her breath warm on his bare chest. She looked up. "I had to see you...after everything that happened...after nearly—"

His arms tightened their hold with her unfinished sentence, too many years of repressed emotion flaring within. Damnation. He didn't need reminding that he'd almost lost her.

"I came here to talk," she said. "To explain."

His pulse kicked up a gear, his chest compressing tightly. Her anger he could endure—but her trust? It might well be the last nail in the coffin to his heart. "I don't expect...you don't need—"

"I do." Her stare was oddly imploring. "Please."

He sucked in a painful breath. Raising a hand, his knuckles gently outlined one side of her face. "Of course."

She nodded and he stepped aside and opened the pool gate, motioning her inside to a bench seat. Aqua water sparkled beneath the muted light of a tall lamp, and down along the harbor, lights blinked and glowed.

They sat side by side, their bodies touching and yet emotionally worlds apart.

She stared off into the distance and he waited silently. He realized she'd find it tough to detail her history, relive it.

Finally, she cleared her throat. "Max was a young man, perhaps twenty, when my father hired him almost a decade ago." She paused, her thumbs fidgeting over her interlaced fingers.

"Go on," he encouraged.

She took a breath. "At some point along the line, he stopped being an employee, and became almost part of the family."

Almost, but not quite. Cray didn't need a psychology degree to imagine how that would have affected a man who was perhaps already close to the edge.

"Max looked out for me and for a short time it felt...nice." She sighed, her slim shoulders rigid and yet fragile against the tiny straps of her black dress.

Cray drew her close. "What happened?"

Her head came to rest on his shoulder. "It was the anniversary of my mother's death. Max came to comfort me." She shrugged. "I was hungry for affection—for love, of any kind."

Cray scowled into the darkness. Max was nothing but a predator. He swept her a long look. "He found you at your lowest ebb and took advantage."

"If I hadn't been intimate with him he'd never have—"

"What, tried to kill you as well?" He took a long, deep breath. Just the thought of that man trying to harm Loretta churned his gut like a spin cycle. "He was an adult obsessed with a woman who didn't return his feelings. That's hardly your fault."

She sighed and he felt her tension ease. "I guess...I guess you're right."

"Where was your dad when Max came looking for you?"

She blinked hard then examined the dark night sky. "He'd left that morning on some urgent business. I knew better though."

She swiped a hand over her face. "Their wedding anniversary, Mum's birthday...he always made himself absent after she died. All those memories, it hurt too much for him to be home."

Cray frowned. That would have offered no comfort to a grieving young girl. A child who'd witnessed her mother's abduction. He didn't know the whole story but he knew she'd been home when kidnappers had stormed the Shaw house and taken Kaitlin, her mum.

Loretta had opened up about Max, perhaps now was the time for her to release a little of her burden about her mum. "What do you remember about your mum's disappearance?"

Her shoulders drooped and her stare fell, her voice low and distant. "I don't remember a lot. But the men who broke in wore masks. They ignored me. I stood frozen, unable to move."

She spoke without emotion and Cray realized that shock still paralyzed her, all these years later.

"They took Mum captive, and I watched as she kicked and struggled. Her screams were muffled by something they'd pushed into her mouth."

His heart twisted. He hated having her relive the pain but, as with a splinter buried deep and spreading infection, she had to get it out. "If you hadn't stayed silent and still, you might very well have been taken too."

But she didn't seem to hear him. Instead her eyes stared out over the city lights. "They dragged her outside and finally I made myself follow. From the doorway, I watched them shove her into a van with black windows. They didn't even spare me a glance as they took off, tires squealing."

His muscles clenched with the futile need to track down the animals who'd taken away Loretta's mother and emotionally tortured an innocent little girl. "I'm sorry," he rasped. "Sweetheart, I truly am."

"I waited and waited. But they...she never came back."

Lincoln had told Cray that he'd found his daughter some two or three hours after the kidnapping. She'd stood in the doorway, frozen and silent.

Apparently she'd been questioned. But through everybody's cajoling and coaxing, she'd not uttered a word.

Cray stifled the urge to soothe the taut lines of her slender body, somehow heal her emotional wounds. But he couldn't yet. She needed to cleanse the torment eating at her soul. He should know. He understood firsthand the suffering endured by losing family.

"You can't blame yourself." He needed her to open up and accept her loss. Grieve for her mother. Yell and scream if need be.

"I let those horrible people take my mother," she said woodenly. "The same people who sent a ransom note three days later, demanding an outrageous sum of money."

He knew Lincoln had paid the money. But he needed her to spill the story, accept what had happened. "Your dad wouldn't have given up on her."

"No." A bitter line pulled at the corners of her lush mouth. "Dad agreed with their terms. The kidnappers responded by delivering three large parcels, with pieces of Mum inside each one."

Cray had seen more in his century life span than most mortals could imagine. What she'd gone through was a horror he knew few would contemplate. Or survive. He'd heard it had taken over a year before she talked again.

"I didn't see those parcels. But I saw Dad's grief, felt an anguish all my own. And I finally came to realize that loving someone, needing a person...well, it's just too painful, too scary."

His heart melted. "Thank you," he said softly. For trusting me. But a sickening despair chased away any trace of optimism. Her blind faith wouldn't spare her from further pain.

He was cursed, never to be free.

Chapter Ten

Loretta's jade-green eyes glistened, her inner beauty reflected in her soulful stare. The male in him shouted adoration, a devotion that had nothing whatsoever to do with his guardian role.

Her stare widened. Her lips parted. And as she turned to him fully, his head swooped, their lips meeting on a breathless sigh. He cupped her face, deepening a kiss that was more about a sharing of their souls than even the physical need soaring between them.

She whimpered beneath his mouth and pressed closer against him, the friction of her body beneath the satiny-soft dress driving him slowly mad with need. When she slipped a hand low to stroke his arousal, he knew without a doubt there would be no turning back.

Blood rushed to his cock and he growled before he wrenched his head back and said thickly, "I told myself this wouldn't happen again."

"And I told myself it would," she countered in a whisper. "I want you." Her eyes glinted when her hand moved to cradle his swollen balls. As she filled her palm with their weight his breath whistled from between clenched teeth.

"And if having you now is our last time together," she reiterated, "then—"

He pressed an unsteady finger to her lips. He couldn't think upon the possibility of their separation, much less hear it. Not right now.

Loretta half-smiled when his hand turned over, his knuckles grazing her parted lips and following the contour of her porcelain-smooth cheek. He clasped her nape and drew her closer still and they kissed with a slow, aching tenderness that turned his blood from a simmer into a boil.

"You're right," she murmured against his mouth. "We've said enough this night." With a decisive touch, she scored her nails into the flesh of his scrotum before trekking a torturous path to the base of his cock.

He hissed with pleasure-pain, shivering reflexively as she clasped his hard length and began to stroke up and down.

Hot damn.

Something fierce, primitive and altogether too possessive burned from him from the inside out. That she even wanted to touch him in his repulsive gargoyle form, worshipped him as if he were some sexy Adonis, undid him in ways nothing else ever could.

His wings unfurled from where they were tucked close to his spine. The tips fluttered, fanning the air above and reminding him only too well of his ugly deformities. *Shit.* What was he thinking? He needed to be human. Now.

He put a hand over Loretta's. She paused then released him. Cray gritted his teeth while his fingers twitched. The urge to press her hand back around his cock robbed him of all rational thought. But regaining a little composure, he at last made a move to climb to his feet.

"No." Her open hand rested against his heart and she pressed him back. "Don't," she said huskily. "Please, don't change."

"I'm a gargoyle, you cannot want—"

"You're wrong. I most definitely do." She reached up, the pads of her fingers tracing a path over his shoulders, down his spine a little, then partway along the rib of his upper wings. "I want you—all of you—just exactly as you are." Her gaze shone. "You're incredible."

He reeled within, the last of his defenses crumbling into ashes. She touched him in places that weren't all on the outside. But it was bittersweet and made all the more poignant knowing their time together couldn't possibly last.

He subsided against the bench seat, swallowing hard. He'd take whatever pleasure and joy Loretta offered, remember the ecstasy long after his curse forced them apart and ground the shattered pieces of his heart into dust.

Like a graceful wraith she slipped off the seat and went onto her knees between his thighs. She looked up, and his heart flip-flopped at her open expression, her gloriously beautiful face.

"I want to pleasure you," she all but purred. "I want to taste you."

He growled with delight as she bent and drew the head of his cock into her mouth, her scarlet-painted lips sealing him in. His hips thrust forward, emitting another guttural groan as her tongue scraped a moist circle around the slitted apex. Then, as though his dick were some delicious Popsicle she couldn't get enough of, couldn't devour quickly enough, she sucked it into her heart-shaped mouth almost to the base.

Her tongue flicked along the thick vein behind his shaft and he closed his eyes with a savagely indrawn breath. Heat built inside him like a pressure boiler ready to explode and he knew he had only seconds before he did exactly that. "Stop."

The cool night air replaced the satin heat of her mouth and he gulped in another lungful of oxygen, forcing his eyes open to see her sitting back on her haunches, her stare fever bright.

He held out his hands and she clasped them, allowing him to pull her up and into his arms. Pushing to his feet he carried her with long strides away from the lamp's glaring arc of light and into the privacy of the shadows.

He knew she'd see little more than the glow of his eyes, his dark silhouette. She'd understand that this dim intimacy wasn't just to shield him and their lovemaking from anyone who might chance upon them, the night cloaked his grotesque physical abnormalities from her too.

A breeze stirred her hair, carrying with it her sweet, flowery scent. She leaned forward, holding his face and murmuring, "Next time we make love, I want to see you. See all of you, my gargoyle lover."

He nodded, his heart jolting once, twice in his chest. Would there even be a next time?

Her lips were petal-soft beneath his as they kissed again, and he savored the peaches and cream taste, basked in the warmth of her silken skin, her sighs.

He drew his head back and she stood motionless, more than a little breathless as one by one, he freed the pearl buttons at the bodice of her designer dress. When she raised her arms, he pulled it up past her shoulders and over her head.

It slithered, unnoticed, from his grasp to somewhere at their feet. He drank his fill of her. In barely there black lace panties, sheer stockings and transparent bra, he knew in all his years he'd never known a woman as sexy, as hot, and as unashamedly passionate as his Loretta.

With deliberate slowness, she bent down and started to draw off her stilettos.

"No, leave them on."

She stilled at his request. Straightening, she reached behind to unclip her bra. "Allow me," she said, her voice as thick and rich as liqueur over ice.

Her bra dropped onto the ground and when she stepped out of her panties Cray was only vaguely aware of the blast of a car horn in the distance, the faint snatches of music and laughter from a party in full swing.

With a ragged groan he moved forward. His hands spanned her waist and, as he carefully lowered her onto the ground, his wings snapped wide then curled around her in a makeshift blanket.

His cock twitched, impossibly harder as her legs fell open with invitation, her glistening core wet just for him.

He moved over her slowly, relishing every inch of her silken skin—her thighs, her taut belly, the round globes of her breasts with their nipples puckering against his chest. Resting his weight on one extended forearm, he palmed the mound of her pussy, opened her secret folds and dipped one finger deep inside.

She moaned and squirmed underneath him, her thighs opening wider still when he pressed deeper inside, his thumb rolling the nub of her clit.

Her back arched and he felt her tighten. God, she was so wet, so slick, already on the precipice of orgasm. It was almost enough to send him over the edge as well.

Her eyes became heavy-lidded, glazed with lust and something much more intimate. She bared her body for him, made him hard and eager. But it was the unveiling of her soul, her feelings laid out for him like a sacrificial lamb, that thickened his cock with desire and made his heart thump with anguish.

Sweet mother of mercy! He looked like a monster—was he acting like one too?

In one abrupt motion he jolted to his feet, his wings bringing her right along with him. And as the curves of her delicious body stamped along his, he had to force himself not to touch her all over. Not yet.

"Is being with me, fucking me—a gargoyle—really what you want?" he growled.

Her brow creased. "Why would you even need to ask?"

"You put your trust in me. That's an honor I cannot abuse twice." His knuckles cracked as his hands fisted at his sides. *Shit*. He was screwing this up. Big time. He really had to work on his deep-and-meaningfuls.

Her face paled. Her eyes shimmered. When his wings slapped open to release her and she stumbled backward, it was pure reflex for him to reach out, keeping her steady until she regained her balance.

She shook her head. "Don't let go. Not now." She took a step toward him and her jutting nipples swiped his chest with every agitated breath. "Don't you ever let me go again!"

She raised her chin, awaiting his response. Except all speech seemed to have dispersed somewhere inside his throat as a flood of emotion caught him unawares, inundating his senses and filling his heart with unattainable longing.

"Cray!"

He refocused on the fiery, passionate woman before him. God, he adored her. "You know I can't promise you that."

She heaved a breath but didn't retreat. Quite the contrary. "Then just...fuck me. Please."

He felt the corners of his mouth lift. Hot damn, she was sexy. And so very proud, wearing nothing more than her high heels. She tilted her hips with deliberate provocation and his dick jolted at the sensation of her belly scraping the head.

He placed a hand at one side of her temple, strands of her soft hair slipping between his fingers as she leaned into his clasp. Even now, she was so trusting, so warm. His other hand slipped down the length of her spine, cupping the rounded curves of her ass. "I'd love to."

Never would he have thought he'd say the word "love" in quite this context. Still, he wasn't about to complain.

She wound her hands around his neck and their mouths came together, their lips meshing, tasting, their tongues entwining. He kept right on kissing as he moved forward, pressing her back until the glass panel of the pool fence forced them to a halt.

She pulled her mouth from his and grinned up at him, shamelessly aroused. "Mm...caught between a cock and a hard place. I like it."

Grasping her ass cheeks, he hoisted her higher. She yelped then sighed a little before wrapping her legs around his hips, the slit of her pussy skimming the tip of his cock. He rotated his pelvis, using the head of his cock to rub her sensitized flesh.

Her stare turned dazed, and she closed her eyes for just a second or two, as if fighting for control.

He understood only too well. Their emotional journey had manifested into a profound, physical need that was unstoppable. Inevitable. He'd been crazy to think he could put a halt to their cravings. Crazy to think they could exist side by side without touching, kissing, fucking, ever again.

Inch by slow inch, he allowed her body to slide down over his, the points of her nipples drawing invisible lines over his skin, his rib cage.

His mouth dried. His temple throbbed simultaneously with his cock, which oozed pre-cum as Loretta's curves slithered over his body.

When she gained her stilettoed feet he demanded thickly, "Turn around."

She did so without protest and he pressed a knee between her thighs. She gasped and spread her legs wide, clutching the rim of the fence.

From behind, he nuzzled her throat as one hand cupped her mound. Deft fingers teased the outer lips with its tight, dark curls before he peeled her pussy wide. Pressing kisses along her neck, he strummed her clit, feeling her tense and shift, undulating against his touch.

"You're about to come," he said huskily. "But not yet. I want to show you how to fly."

He lifted her until her buttocks rested low on his stomach. She let out a startled gasp, keeping hold of the pool fence for support.

A fresh wave of heat fired straight through his cock at the press of her white, rounded ass cheeks, the sight of her perfect breasts suspended so very close. He nuzzled her gold-brown hair that flowed like silk along her spine, breathing in the delicate scent of apples and something elusive.

"Do you trust me?" he asked.

Her spine unlocked, her body loosening. "Yes."

He leaned close, licking the shell of her ear before gently nipping the lobe. She moaned then hissed with pleasure as he drove his tongue into her ear. He drew back, his breath fanning her hair. "I won't let you go."

He couldn't promise her a future. But he could promise her this.

His wings unfurled and arced to the front in a semicircle. In one fluid movement he elevated her higher again. She released her grip on the fence as he placed her thighs over his shoulders, her arms draped along his wings.

In this position she really was dangling over a precipice, face first and high in the air, floating, flying. And soon, climaxing.

"Tell me what you see." He needn't tell her of the vista she provided. He had only to crook his neck a little to see her wet pussy with its vee of tight curls.

Her voice shook. "I see infinite darkness, pitch-black night with city lights far below, like sparklers."

"What do you feel?"

She let out a shuddery laugh, her voice strained. "I feel exhilarated, aroused, yet scared I'll fall into the abyss. I feel as if I'm caught right on the edge, between adrenaline and wild orgasm."

He shifted her position slightly, aligning her pussy to his mouth. He scented her musk, but wanted even more to taste it. He licked her exposed pink flesh in one long sweep of his tongue. "And now, what do you feel?"

She didn't—couldn't—answer for a moment. Her breasts rose and fell as she struggled to catch her breath. "I'm...I'm not sure." She shifted, giving his tongue better access. "I think I need an encore," she said breathlessly.

With his wings and shoulders balancing her weight, his hands were free to open her wide as he licked and sucked, focusing on her clit like it was the only thing that mattered.

"Cray!" Her cry of ecstasy was pure, unadulterated abandonment as she abruptly convulsed and he had to grit his teeth against the bolt of lust filling his balls.

She was trembling with aftershocks when he unlatched her thighs from his shoulders. As his wings folded behind his spine, his hands snared hold of her waist and tugged her against him.

She writhed, clearly hot for more. She leaned forward, grasping the fence until her breasts compressed against the glass and his cock strained at the entrance of her damp slit.

She turned her head, her eyes flashing heat. "I need you inside me."

With her sweet cunt kissing the head of his cock, he was in no position to deny her. Couldn't hold back a guttural groan as he thrust forward, his cock plunging deep inside.

Her breath expelled on a gasp. But it was too late now to worry about his gargoyle size.

The tendons in his neck strained. His pulse hammered at the sheer, overwhelming bliss of making love with this woman with the incredibly heightened sensitivity of a gargoyle.

His cock throbbed and through clenched teeth he half sobbed out a breath, his hands bunching into fists as he resisted coming hard and hot inside her. Her inner muscles gloved him, almost undoing him. But somehow he held back as he stroked harder and faster, the slap of flesh hitting flesh almost drowning out Loretta's mewls of delight.

She came hard. Her muscles squeezed his cock, pulling and sucking. As she sobbed out his name like a benediction, he returned the favor, bellowing her name into the night air as he too surrendered to rapture, his seed erupting inside her, filling her, marking her as his. In a haze, he felt her shudder once more, heard her awed and breathless "Wow" as another orgasm took her by surprise.

"Wow indeed," he agreed hoarsely.

She shifted awkwardly, and he reluctantly let her go. His cock slid free as she slipped to the ground. He followed her and gathered her close then flipped them around so that she lay on top of him. His outspread wings tucked her close and warm, and she sighed, happy and replete, before winding her legs around him as if she'd never let go.

As gargoyle, Cray heard the sudden snap of a twig a nanosecond before Lincoln's enraged voice jerked them apart.

"Get the hell away from my daughter."

Chapter Eleven

Cray captured Loretta's hand, drawing her up beside him and shielding her with a wing as he stood and faced her father. Without his wheelchair, Lincoln advanced with jerky steps, which Cray suspected had little to do with old age and everything to do with wrath.

"You broke our pact," Lincoln snarled at him. Leaning against the pool gate, his breathing heavy, he burst out, "And you failed to protect my daughter. You're not fit for the role of guardian."

Loretta gasped. "Daddy! You don't know what you're saying."

Lincoln turned on his daughter and even in the shadows Cray made out the sheen on the elderly man's face, the ugly redness of anger and grief.

"My word, I do, you silly chit!" His eyes blazed. "You could have had Max but instead you drove him mad with your loose morals." He coughed fitfully then drew another ragged breath. "Just weeks ago he asked permission to seek your hand in marriage."

Tension hummed from Loretta like a force field as she faced down her father. "I'm guessing you said yes?"

"Of course. I was—"

"Relieved?" she finished for him.

Lincoln slumped, hacking out another cough. "Bah. You are out of control. Your reputation tattered." He lifted his head slowly, as if it were too heavy for his shoulders. "Frankly, I was surprised he would do you the honor."

Cray's blood ran lava hot. But when Loretta choked out a sob, instant freeze avalanched down his spine. He drew Loretta close, indifferent to her father's withering stare that took in every inch of his gargoyle nakedness. "I'd marry her in a heartbeat, if I could."

Loretta went quiet but he was aware of her galloping pulse, her shuddering breaths. Just as he perceived her dad's all-enveloping rage.

"Of course you would, you monster. You knew Max loved her but you wanted her all for yourself and got rid of the only man who wanted her for more than just her too-willing body."

Loretta's arm snaked around Cray's waist, her body leaning into his as if soaking up its strength. "The only monster I'm seeing, Daddy, is you." She looked up at Cray, her moist stare beseeching as she said softly, "Get me out of here."

They turned toward the cliff face but paused as Lincoln roared, "Retta. Don't you dare leave with him."

She didn't turn around, her spine steely straight as she said, "I can't bear to stay."

"Then you leave me no choice," Lincoln said hoarsely.

Cray half turned and watched as her dad lurched inside the gate, the old man's attention once again focused solely on him.

"I release you, gargoyle. Release you from your guardian role."

Loretta stumbled. "No! No...no...no!"

Cray reached out and steadied her. But his breath hissed at the sudden, heavy weight inside his chest, his belly that twisted with grief. "I'm sorry, Loretta. So very, very sorry," he whispered.

He dropped his hold and stepped away, a little piece of him dying just then at her sob of denial, at the way her splayed arms covered her nudity. But restlessness already tugged at his awareness, a compulsion impossible to ignore. No matter how much he wanted to stay...he couldn't.

His wings unfurled, fluttering in preparation for flight. With fierce resolve he stilled them, arcing the leathery tip of one low before sliding it like a wisp of satin beneath her chin.

Fire burned in her stare, and he knew then she would not for a moment accept this fate. He smiled but he felt no joy. Had he been human, had circumstances been different, he'd have made this amazing woman his wife.

"Goodbye, my darling," he said thickly. "I'll never forget you."

Tears trekked freely down her face. "I'll see you again. Soon," she whispered.

He pivoted away, his eyes stinging, his spirit numb. He wished he could stay even just a little longer. Wished he could voice the three little words scalding his throat.

But wishes weren't for the likes of him.

He lunged into a sprint toward the cliff, almost oblivious to the wetness spilling down his cheeks. He leapt over the glass fencing and into the abyss on the other side. Freefalling, he gave into the gut-wrenching howl of anguish he could no longer contain.

Chapter Twelve

Loretta watched the sun slowly sink behind the ocean's horizon. It cast a blood-red path all the way to the shore, turning the creamy froth of gentle waves a luminous pink.

She let out a shaky breath, trying hard to concentrate on its beauty and maintain the numbness she'd embraced these last two months since Cray's enforced leave, and then her father's sudden death just three days later.

She hadn't been completely insensate. She'd had the foresight to hire a professional to track down Cray—a satellite surveillance technician at the top of his game.

Like it or not, being the sole benefactor to an empire had its advantages.

It was truly unbelievable that Cray had only been a hop, skip and jump away—a twenty-minute drive south from the harbor mansion if the traffic was flowing.

The sun dipped fully behind the sea and she stepped back into the shadows, at last giving in to the shiver of excitement that evoked once more what it was to feel alive.

Finally she'd be reunited with Cray.

"You shouldn't be here."

She spun around, giddy with relief and wild optimism. Her heart thrashed in her chest as she grinned like a loon. She might not be able to see him but she heard the longing in his voice, the need. "You surely didn't think I'd stay away?" she asked huskily.

At the silence, she took a few steps forward. Her night vision adjusted and she finally made out his looming silhouette just yards away.

Tingles shot down her spine, raising goose bumps along the flesh of her arms. She'd almost forgotten just how big he was. How charismatic. "You surely didn't think I'd forget about us, did you?" she added in a whisper.

She brushed a hand over her belly. God willing, there was even more reason now for them to be together.

His eyes glinted. "No. No I—"

A sharp crack—a gunshot?—cut his sentence short. He grunted in surprise and staggered backward. An instant later he appeared to regain his bearings. Looking up, he said harshly, "Run!"

"But you—" She didn't—couldn't—move as the world suddenly spun crazily around her. She swallowed back the panicked waves of dizziness "You've been shot."

A bullet thudded into the ground close by as another crack sounded, sending up a spray of sand.

With a fierce expletive, Cray charged toward her. Without breaking stride he scooped her into his arms. His wings curled forward, shielding her. Bending low, his mouth close to her ear, he hissed, "Stay quiet. Don't do anything to regain their attention."

Loretta bit back a sob. Emotions she'd kept locked away now spilled free, escalating and running rampant in her mind. She'd thought fate had dealt her its worst blow with her mother's kidnapping, Max's madness and her father's death.

It hadn't.

Cray had been hurt. And with his guardian instincts kicking into gear and shoving all self-preservation aside, he might very well not survive this night.

"Hold on tight," he whispered urgently.

She did so without a word, twining her hands behind his neck, her legs around his waist. She felt his muscles bunch then he leapt high into the air, his wings unfurling wide.

In the darkness, she made out the blurred silhouette of a large tree and just yards away a huge house. Leaves quivered as Cray grabbed hold of a thick tree branch. When he swung onto it, she felt the strain in his body, heard his nearly inaudible gasp of pain.

"Are you okay?" she asked.

His mouth covered hers in a hard, desperate kiss, silencing her. Yet his voice was gentle, almost poignant as he whispered, "Stay here. Please." His voice thrummed with tension and then a tinge of self-mockery when he added almost inaudibly, "Duty calls."

He placed her on the branch, and even in the darkness she saw him wince, knew he was badly wounded. "You'll be safe now. Just. Don't. Move." He looked at her hard, and then curved a hand around her head.

His touch lingered then dropped. And without a backward glance he hoisted himself higher into the tree. Something wet splattered onto her arm. She touched it, her hand coming away sticky and wet. Blood, she realized with a soundless moan.

Through the branches, a half-moon glimmered between parting clouds, enabling her to see Cray as he dropped into a crouch above. He paused then vaulted across the gap. Landing nimbly on the pitched roof ledge, he disappeared up and over its other side.

She sucked in a breath and released it. But panic suffused her from the inside out, making her teeth chatter and her hands visibly shake.

It was happening all over again. She was going to lose the one person who meant the world to her. Her stomach cramped, her skin felt hot, as if it were on fire, while she fought off a need to throw up.

Please...not again.

But her silent plea went unheard as she saw sudden movement in the shadows below. Three shapes materialized into men from out of the darkness. Dangerous, heavily armed men, she realized with a hastily covered gasp as moonlight glinted on one of the firearms.

Dizziness hit again and receded. She wanted to yell out, to warn Cray of the approaching danger. But no words could pass through the thick lump wedged in her throat.

Oh God.

She couldn't stand back and watch the one she loved die.

Not this time.

Chapter Thirteen

Cray dropped into the front courtyard. From there he could view the road and a small section of beach from where the bullets had been fired.

Clouds drifted over the moon once more but it mattered little. The radar of his gargoyle senses was attuned to Loretta—taking away his focus, distracting him from the life-and-death issues at hand.

His breath hissed. *Damn it.* He had to concentrate.

A sudden breeze cooled his skin, bringing a faint whiff of his attacker. His nose crinkled with distaste. Sweat. And fear.

He heard footsteps. More than one attacker, he realized with a flare of alarm. But it was an anxiety held for Loretta alone.

His new guardianship status hardly registered.

He had no time to ponder this inconceivable development. Adam, the criminal lawyer he'd guarded since he'd been forced to leave Loretta, would be close to pissing his pants right now.

He grimaced. The sooner he rescued the unlikable little man, the sooner he could get back to Loretta and make certain she didn't get hurt.

Cray turned around and faced a large wooden door. Its delicate carvings didn't fool him into doubting its solid construction but with no time to key in a security code, he raised his foot high and lashed out.

The door burst open, splinters of wood skidding into the entrance foyer. A high-tech alarm screamed to life.

He hoped the noise would distract the attackers—even give them good reason to withdraw but knew it was unlikely. What they had planned would be completed before any police or security guard checked out the disturbance.

He raced up the stairs. The wound in his shoulder burned like fury. Blood freely spilled, splattering the fine cream-colored wool carpet.

He didn't need to use his refined senses to find the man the thugs were really after. The fancy criminal lawyer was blubbering and hysterical, cowering beneath his four-poster bed in a rumpled business suit.

Cray dragged Adam out with his good arm, the other one now almost useless. "Quiet," he snapped.

"But...they're coming for me. I heard the gunshots outside!" The lawyer's face was blotchy red as he stumbled forward. Arms pin-wheeling, he grabbed hold of Cray and one hand curled like a vise on his guardian's injured shoulder. "You have to help me."

Cray almost howled with pain and when Adam's fingers dug even deeper into his wound he gritted his teeth and carefully extracted the lawyer's torturous grip. With a well-aimed strike, he cracked him a good one across the skull.

Adam crumpled to the floor without another word and Cray murmured without remorse, "It's safer this way, for both of us."

He gathered the unconscious man into his arms, wincing at the searing agony in his shoulder. He moved toward the window and peered through. No one below. He stepped back. The glass was thick but breakable. And they were high enough to glide to safety.

He paused, adrenaline surging at the light tread climbing fast up the hardwood stairs. He had seconds to escape—

"Cray, wait!"

He turned, hardly able to believe his ears—his eyes—as he faced the one woman who haunted his every dream, his every thought. "No!" He sucked in a breath. "Hide," he rasped.

"Not without you." She took a few steps through the doorway, eyes fierce and head held proudly.

He shifted Adam's weight with his good arm. A vein in his temple throbbed, his heart jumping like a jackhammer on full speed. "You must." Didn't she understand? He couldn't lose her, couldn't live without her.

At the thought, he lost touch with reality, lost touch with everything around him so that when his head cleared and he finally detected the muzzle of a gun pointed at him from the doorway, it was too damn late to react.

Too late to realize Loretta's intention as she turned and leapt toward the attacker with a shrill cry.

And like someone watching their own worst nightmare, he saw her jerk to a stop at the muffled crack of the gunshot, heard her breath catch as she fell with infinite slowness to her knees.

Chapter Fourteen

Loretta knew she was in the hospital. The smell of antiseptic hit her nostrils and as she moved an arm, hot pain tore through her body like barbed wire jerked backward.

But it was her gargoyle she sensed above the burning agony and she strove to push through the last heavy layers of consciousness to force open gritty eyes.

The bustling sounds of activity immediately receded as she focused on Cray. Half-open curtains framed him in a halo of sunlight, its warmth caressing his whiskered cheeks, his brow and its white puckered scar.

Impossible! A strangled cry burst from her lips. And in human form, Cray jerked awake from where he'd slumped in a chair that was too small for his large frame.

"I don't believe it," she choked out.

He was by her side in a nanosecond. He reached over and pressed the nurse-call button. "It's true," he said hoarsely, brushing a cool hand over her fevered brow. "You saved my life...and broke the curse."

All thoughts jammed and then bounced around her mind like the steel orb in a pinball machine. She wished she could rejoice and shout for joy. She couldn't. Instead, she closed her eyes and weathered an overwhelming swell of anxiety.

Her greatest wish had now become her greatest fear. He was a free man now. Free to stay—or go.

"Hey, what's wrong?" he asked softly.

Everything. Nothing.

She opened her eyes. "What happens now?" she asked, wincing at the searing pain in her shoulder that trapped her immobile on the hospital bed.

"Sh." He pressed a gentle hand to her lips. "We'll talk later," he murmured. "For now, you need to rest."

"But what about those men with guns?"

"Don't worry, they won't ever hurt you again."

She sighed, weariness pressing around her. "You killed them?"

"No." She heard an edge of regret in his voice. "All three are in the hospital too, under police guard." His chair creaked. The pad of his thumb drifted over one side of her face. "I'm betting the officers don't quite know what to make of their tale," he murmured, darkness coloring his dry amusement.

A nurse came in and they fell silent while her wound-free arm was cuffed to check her blood pressure. Loretta's eyelids fluttered closed, and even before the nurse had finished, she felt herself drifting back into the folds of sleep.

The very next day she was discharged, the doctors happy with her recovery. She was just happy to leave the sterile place with the virile Cray by her side.

Not that he was full of talk, but then, neither was she. It was just nice to look out the passenger window as the townhouses and trees zoomed past. Only one he slowed the car and keyed in a code to activate the security gates to a tall, luxury apartment building, did she shift a little restlessly in the passenger seat.

Her breath caught in her throat as she watched his somber expression. Was this where he'd gently break the news and tell her that he wanted his freedom?

He drove the car down a steep ramp and into underground parking.

"Where are we?" she asked, a lump in her throat.

"I thought you might like to see my home."

"Oh...yes." He had his own place?

He parked the car and got out. His footsteps were a muffled staccato on the concrete as he walked around and opened the passenger door before bending low and gathering her close.

"I'm f-fine to walk," she said, sounding breathless and more than a little unsteady as he hoisted her effortlessly into his arms.

"Humor me."

"But what about you? I saw the blood. There was so much…"

He shrugged. "What can I say? The bullet went clean through muscle and bone, and we gargoyles heal fast."

"So you're still gargoyle?"

"Yes. But it's no longer involuntary. I can change at will."

"I'm glad."

"Really?" he asked with a raised brow, clearly unconvinced.

"Yes! Even with wings, you're more human than many people I know."

A sigh shuddered from him. "I'm pleased you think so."

A little thrill arrowed down to her toes. "So, you're a true shape shifter now?" At his nod, she probed, "Are you aware of any other changes?"

He managed a shrug. "Not that I'm aware of. Though whether or not I age now, or am still immortal, remains to be seen."

He paused at a wall with huge shiny metal doors. On a keypad he entered identification and it dawned on her that they were at a private elevator.

"I own the building," he said before she could formulate the question. The doors swished open and he stepped inside. "I lease it out but the penthouse suite is all mine."

The doors closed and little red numbers flashed as the elevator shot them smoothly skyward. She lifted a hand and smoothed her hair, oddly self-conscious. The close confines of the elevator heightened the simmering awareness that was a constant between them.

She closed her eyes and absorbed his heartbeat, profoundly grateful that she was in his arms as giddy anticipation filled her.

There had been so very many men in her life but none like her gargoyle. With Cray, she wanted to scratch far below the surface, uncover the real Cray, the man and everything in between.

But could he forget her past? Her lashes flicked up. "All those men, they meant nothing—"

"I know." He wound a piece of her hair around his finger and tucked it behind her ear. "You had many lovers," he agreed. "You were seeking affection but in all the wrong places."

Emotion welled in her chest. A single tear trickled down her cheek. He brushed it away with the pad of his thumb and added huskily, "You used sex to fill a void. I understand."

"Why do you care now?" she asked thickly. "You made it clear you were nothing more than my guardian."

"I do care. Very much," he said quietly.

The elevator stopped, the doors opened. But they didn't alight. Her pulse skittered but she quickly banished wishful thinking. So why this jagged hole in her chest where her heart should be?

"I cared that you were hurting. I cared that every time your father saw you, he was reminded of the wife he mourned. Lincoln abandoned you at a time when you needed him most," Cray said, his expression resolute beneath the dim overhead light. "But it's time for you to move on, accept that what happened to your mother was never your fault."

Breath wheezed in and out of her lungs. "How can I? I did nothing to help her. Nothing."

He stared at her hard. "You were a child. It was nobody's fault but the kidnappers." His face softened. "Your father focused on work to erase the pain. He didn't consider your hurt too."

A strangled sound tore from deep in her chest. Cray was right. She'd shouldered the brunt of her mum's disappearance, and not one person had ever told her it wasn't her fault. Until Cray.

Another whimper escaped. His words had liberated the shackled piece of her, freed the constant, dull ache trapped deep inside. It seared through her mind, tearing at the foundations of her belief.

His arms were hard and strong around her, propping her against the solid safety of his chest while she heaved gut-wrenching breaths.

"Dad blamed me for not looking out for M-Mom."

Cray's chin rested on her head, his breath warm on her scalp. "No. You blamed yourself, sweetheart. Lincoln was so full of his own guilt for not protecting his family, he couldn't comprehend how you felt."

She wrapped her good arm around the back of his neck. Her fingers twined through his thick hair. "I know…I know you're right," she whispered.

"Then let the past go," he said huskily.

She drew in a heavy breath then gave a shaky nod and looked up. "Wh-what about you? You must miss your family?"

His eyes darkened. "Yes."

His cheek rasped beneath her palm. "Yet you've been alive so long."

Did the pain of loss never disappear?

His eyes flashed, revealing the emotional wounds that ran deep. Another shadow veiled his gaze. "I'll never forget my family. I can't lie—I still miss them very much."

"I hope you at least had a chance to say goodbye."

His shoulders bunched. "No. I wasn't able to."

"The curse?"

"Yes. I was forced to leave England, compelled to guard an apathetic, European prince. Not long afterward, my parents and little sister died from diphtheria."

Emotion clogged her throat. She'd endured much death too. But to lose a whole family while bound to protect someone you didn't care about? No wonder he understood her, understood her guilt and pain.

"Cray, I'm so very sorry." She meant it with every shard of her being.

Something passed between them, a shared understanding. Then, as if collecting himself, he strode through the elevator doors. Automated lights flooded on, dazzling them, and the moment was gone.

He set her gently onto her feet. And suddenly everything seemed awkward, contrived, as if they were young lovers experimenting with sex for the first time.

"Can I get you a drink?" he asked brusquely.

"Please." She followed him to a cedar bar.

"Scotch, vodka?"

"Scotch. Thank you."

Even when he was fully dressed in jeans and a white dress shirt, she couldn't help but admire his body as he bent and selected a bottle from the lower shelf. He was built like an athlete. Wide shoulders, long, muscular legs and a flat stomach with a washboard ripple.

As he splashed the amber liquid into squat glasses, she asked, "Why did you bring me here? Why now?" When he turned, eyes hooded as he handed her the drink, she urged, "Tell me. Please."

He took a swallow and then placed his glass back onto the bar. "I didn't plan it. But I realized you didn't want to go home...you never were comfortable there."

He'd known! The harbor mansion had never felt welcoming. She'd always felt like an outsider looking in, never quite fitting into the world her father had expected her to inhabit.

She placed her untouched drink by his, studying his unreadable face. "You're right. But so what?" She needed to hear how he felt without having to always second-guess him.

"You want me to spell it out?" he growled. "Want me on my knees, groveling?"

"It would make a nice change," she said, deadpan.

His expression shifted and suddenly he threw his head back and let out a deep belly laugh, the sound rich and pleasurable as it rolled off his tongue and bounced off the pristine walls. His stare glittered, eyes eating her up. "Touché."

She didn't say a word, just stared and stared. Then he abruptly dropped onto his knees, his face open and letting her know it was her move.

She didn't need coaxing. She moved toward him and he opened his arms, drawing her against him. His mouth lifted to meet hers and they kissed softly at first, exploring each other with tender restraint.

He pulled back a little, looking into her eyes with utter seriousness. "I have to ask you one last time because, God help me, I'll never have the courage to ask again—is this what you want? Am I what you want?"

Loretta stepped back. "Yes." *Oh yes.* She licked her swollen lower lip, eyeing his heat-stoked gaze, his sensual mouth. He was giving her control.

She lifted a hand, tracing the jagged scar along his brow and realizing it would be a permanent reminder for him of his human days long ago, before he'd become indestructible.

He must surely know she loved everything about him. His flaws were just a small part of his beautiful package. "I want no one else. Just...you."

Chapter Fifteen

Loretta heard Cray's breath hiss, and suddenly they were in each other's arms again, their mouths fused while each peeled the clothes frantically off the other.

Time was a luxury they had now, with Cray freed from his curse. But their hunger was urgent, primal, needy.

With their clothes scattered around them, he stood and propelled her backward, the wall suddenly against her spine. She eagerly wrapped her legs around his hips, emitting a gasp when the head of his cock nudged her slit, opening her to his sex.

He thrust forward and her head abruptly rocked back, a cry of pleasure-pain tearing from her lips as he filled her to the hilt.

He held the position for just a few seconds but it seemed long minutes as she writhed in his hold, so very desperate for more. He pulled back, the head of his cock just barely nudging her slick entrance, and she almost shrieked with the need to have him back inside her.

His ice blue stare anything but cold, he flashed a look that was wholly possessive as he demanded throatily, "Tell me you want me."

Her chest heaved as she fought for breath, her breasts quivering. "I want you," she gasped. And she knew as only a lover would—this time he wanted her to beg, not reassure.

His cock sank into her pussy a few inches, the cords along his neck straining. "I'm not sure I heard," he grated out softly.

She drew in a breath, her nostrils flaring in response. The scent of male, of sex and passion, had her almost coming from arousal alone. "I want you! I want you so bad it almost hurts. I want all of you inside me!"

He smiled, triumphant. And with a barely contained groan, he thrust his cock fully inside her, the walls of her pussy clutching then releasing as he pounded a relentless rhythm that caught them up and held them as one, suspending them in a world where nothing else mattered, where only they existed.

A climax caught her unawares, holding her in its grip for a beat, before tossing her high, to a faraway place where her every pleasure crystallized then shattered and reformed again. She screamed out his name, her toes curling as she convulsed around him, Cray groaning loud and long as he shuddered his release deep inside her.

She became aware once more of her surroundings, heard the almost silent whir of air-conditioning, the deep tick-tock of a nearby grandfather clock.

With a stunned sigh, she ran the back of her hand over Cray's shoulders, over his pecs and down along his abs. She smiled dreamily as he caught his breath in pleasure, his chest compressing.

She felt boneless, weightless as she swiveled her head to where huge windows showcased the city below and an endless horizon. Daylight had long since melted away. Now dusk breathed tinges of pink and gold into the air.

Loretta turned back, crooking her neck to watch the man above her. God, she didn't want to lose him. She ran an abstract hand over her still-flat belly as emotion rose and swelled inside, snatching her breath and causing her pulses to jump.

Could she risk it all? Could she not? Could she truly be happy living without telling this man how she felt? No. Better to risk losing him than pretend such feelings didn't exist. Better to risk his rejection by telling him their lovemaking had created a life that grew day by day inside her.

He leaned down, pressing a long, tender kiss to her lips. She smiled tentatively then unhooked her legs. Taking his hand, she led him to the glazed, floor-to-ceiling sliding doors and outside onto the patio. Pink and gold had smeared together, the sky blushed apricot.

"Beautiful," he whispered, but he looked only at her.

"It's a big world out there," she said. "And now you have your freedom—"

"I want you more than ever."

When she swung toward him, he said throatily, "I love you. I want to spend the rest of my life with you. I don't care where that is."

"You really mean that?" she breathed.

"Yes. More than anything." He curved a hand beneath her chin. "The night you were shot, when you put your life on the line for me, I surrendered to my feelings. I listened to my heart, which I'd ignored far too long." His smile was filled with wonder and rich with warmth. "Only then did love break the curse."

Her mind whirred. He really loved her! She allowed a moment of unparalleled joy. Her eyes held his. "But...how?"

His hand scraped a path along her jaw and down her throat. "I don't really know. But the moment I was no longer compelled to guard a mortal, it was as if a fog that clouded my mind had suddenly lifted. Somehow I just knew I wouldn't be turning to stone come sunrise."

All this time he'd been trying to protect them both by rejecting how they felt. It truly was a miracle that he had embraced their deeper feelings.

He loved her, she realized yet again. She felt like a flower bursting open at dawn. "I love you too," she said. "I've always loved you."

A sound rumbled from deep in his chest. When it burst from his throat, it was unlike anything she'd heard. It was desperate joy and rising hope.

She swallowed. "Cray?" His expression went somber as her smile wobbled at the corners. "I think you'll make a great dad."

His mouth tightened. He dragged a hand through his short hair. "I'm sorry to turn your dreams to dust but that's not going to happen."

He didn't want to be a dad? Her heart sank, pain searing through her veins. No. She refused to believe he'd be anything but a fantastic father. She stepped closer, snaring his forearm. "You can learn. Together, we'll make it happen."

"Loretta." Despair burned at the back of his eyes. "I'm sterile." He turned away for a moment, clearly gathering his thoughts. "And even if it was possible, I still carry gargoyle DNA…"

"Cray, I'm pregnant."

His eyes went wide, his jaw rigid. Her teeth pricked her lower lip as she whispered, dry-mouthed, "I've thought of all the worst-case scenarios, but no more. Our child will be healthy and happy—"

"And loved dearly," Cray finished, taking hold of her waist and lifting her high as he let out an amazed whoop. With sudden care he placed her back onto her feet, his face beaming, incredulous as he asked, "You're sure? About the baby, I mean."

She nodded, and he folded her into his arms and held her tight, his breath warm on her scalp, his heart galloping against her cheek.

Stars lit up the sky like a chandelier when he at last released her and voiced once more, "I love you. God, how I love you."

She giggled, heady with emotion as he abruptly changed into gargoyle. He climbed over the safety rail and held out his arms, his wings fluttering lazily behind.

"It's a beautiful night." He stretched out a hand. "Come explore it with me."

"No duty, no curse. Just us?"

He wrapped her close. "Yes. Together. Forever."

Want more Winged & Dangerous stories from Mel Teshco...
Ice Cold Lover

Celeste Diamond has a secret she will fight tooth and nail to protect. She is human in every way but one—hideous bat-like wings, a permanent legacy from her once-cursed gargoyle father, Cray. But she is seriously attracted to Pascal Daniels, despite him being the son of a mobster, and every woman's most dangerous fantasy.

Pascal Daniels is used to attention from women, but he's looking for someone special. He's fascinated by the ice queen, Celeste Diamond. He thinks hers is the perfect female form, one he'd do anything to possess. Pascal has decided it's way past time to warm up the mysterious, elusive Celeste.

And perhaps he'll share some secrets of his own.

Chapter One of Ice Cold Lover

The smell of money, and lots of it, permeated the air of the Sydney casino as Celeste Diamond stepped out of the elevator and onto its lavish third floor. Booked exclusively for invitation-only guests, it was here the rich and powerful, the famous and not-so-famous, came to flaunt their splendor.

She scarcely noticed. Instead, every one of her senses isolated the man who'd gone to great lengths this last month—with little success—to get to know her.

Pascal Daniels was a name synonymous to power and wealth, with murky undercurrents linking him to the seedy underworld of organized crime. Add notorious playboy to the mix and he was one black sheep she'd do well to avoid—if only she wasn't a heartbeat away from tearing the clothes right off his magnificent body!

Heat crept up her throat as high-voltage lust zapped straight between her thighs. Her nipples pebbled beneath her white sheath dress and the corset bra under the many layers of gauzy material encircling her torso.

Pascal would never see the physical evidence puckering just for him. The corset disguised more than just her gargoyle wings.

She watched him push to his feet in one smooth, fluid movement. He towered above the blackjack table and a pair of scantily clad women who'd been hanging over him. He ignored them both. Instead, his hot stare feasted on her, swept her up and down like a lover's caress, his attention hers alone.

She swallowed convulsively. When he abandoned his chips with a careless wave, the breath wedged somewhere low in her throat.

Oh, dear god. Am I ready for this?

Her spine snapped tight, subduing the hideous, bat-like appendages quivering beneath their bonds. And for just one moment self-doubt iced the carnal heat flowing like lava in her veins. Would this man be so fascinated if he saw her in all her naked glory, with her unbound wings stretched high and wide?

She'd never give him the chance to find out.

Oh, they'd be intimate this night, except it would be strictly on her terms, when she was ready and not before. She would never be one of his easy conquests.

With slow provocation, she turned her back on him, a gesture that made her shiver even as she burned. Had anyone ever had the nerve to snub this man?

Snatching a flute of champagne from a passing tray, she sipped the bubbles of decadence while dancing her way around the milling crowd of glitterati. She needn't look behind to see if he followed—her every molecule screamed that he did. A gurgle of laughter spilled free, a dizzy excitement from the thrill of the hunt. She hadn't felt so alive, so utterly aroused...ever!

Pascal had awakened something deep inside her, unleashed needs that weren't just physical. He'd stimulated her mentally too. Though she'd kept any dialogue between them brief, she'd discovered a man incredibly complex and intelligent.

A man wholly in control.

"Celeste!" Over the buzz of conversation, the throaty voice of her friend, Lexie, was unmistakable. The dark-haired woman motioned her over to where she was placing bets at a roulette wheel. "I wondered if you would make it," she said with a mock glower, leaning toward her and air kissing each cheek.

Celeste inwardly grimaced, her joy evaporating. Even acquaintances knew better than to touch her. It hurt to know they all imagined her "no-touch policy" was used solely to cultivate her ice-queen image.

They couldn't be more wrong.

"I couldn't resist," she conceded wryly. Then sweeping a look at Lexie's double stack of chips, she murmured, "You're on a winning streak."

Her friend grinned, shamelessly blasé as she swept out a languid, heavily bejeweled hand. "Not at all. I've lost almost everything I came here with."

With Lexie's family owning shipping lines and major foreign media shares, Celeste supposed her friend could afford to be careless. Her lips pursed. One day she'd have that conversation with her about using money in a more altruistic way.

Sudden heat prickled along her nape, blasting philosophical thoughts clean away. Her pulse thudded, every one of her muscles tensing in reaction. Pascal had come to claim her.

Lexie's grin widened, and then became predatory as she peered past her and arched a thinly-plucked brow. "Well, Little Miss Secretive," Lexie turned a speculative gaze her way, "I suspect you won't be going home a loser tonight."

Celeste recognized thinly veiled jealousy when she heard it but didn't rise to the bait. Still, she couldn't help but turn to face the man who'd invaded her dreams and morphed them into something deliciously wicked for twenty-six nights straight.

"Good evening, ladies," Pascal murmured, his husky voice as smooth and fine as a long sip of aged malt whiskey.

Lexie preened, unmistakably a pushover for this man with his handsome face, athlete's body and a charisma that beckoned at twenty paces. Add to his repertoire oodles of charm, power and wealth, and Celeste could almost empathize.

"Mind if I steal your friend?" Pascal asked the dark-haired woman.

"Oh, I'm sure she won't mind," Lexie purred. "It's not as if she's here to gamble."

Pascal quirked a black-as-sin brow and directed a glint of amusement toward Celeste. "Is that so?"

Celeste scowled, and he grinned as if he were the recipient of some fabulous joke. "I believe we make our own luck," she said tightly, "and not by some throw of the dice."

He shrugged, his grin widening. "You may be right." He swept a hand around the room, his jacket cracking open, drawing her gaze to his tanned throat and white dress shirt that hugged the faint ripple of his abs. "Just don't go letting everyone know, hmm? Not everyone shares your obvious...passion."

Breath lodged in her throat. Oh, she felt passion all right. And never before had it burned so fever bright! "I'll keep that in mind," she managed, all too aware of his spicy male scent, his intoxicating nearness.

Lexie winked broadly at Pascal, before turning to her friend with a smirk. "Why did you come tonight? I'm betting it isn't for my scintillating company."

Celeste had learned to despise probing questions almost as much as she did unwanted physical contact. But she'd adapted, outmaneuvering most queries and becoming ambiguous with others. "You're right." She lifted her glass. "I come solely for the pink champagne."

As she swallowed the last of her drink, Pascal's eyes danced with mirth. One corner of his lips tilted. "I imagine you'd come for something more gratifying than that."

Lexie guffawed at the smoothly delivered double entendre, her mind evidently no longer on her friend or the roulette wheel as she raked a suggestive look over his black-suited body. "She mightn't, but I would."

Something toxic and nasty seared Celeste's belly, an emotion she didn't want to examine too closely. Pascal was a hot body, a man to satisfy her insatiable urges—nothing more. Lexie was welcome to him, after Celeste was done with him.

Her womb clenched with anticipation at the mere thought of Pascal's cock buried deep inside her. Then her chest constricted as another image flashed—Lexie entwined with Pascal, her abundant breasts filling his hands, her silken hair wrapped around him like a midnight cloak.

Pascal held out a crooked elbow, pointedly ignoring the other woman's come-on. "May I?"

Placing her empty glass onto a passing waiter's tray, Celeste considered him, faking indecision she certainly didn't feel.

Pascal was obviously familiar with her hands-off rule. She wasn't the infamous "ice queen" for nothing. Then again, had this man ever observed convention? Her pulse kicked into top gear. He was high-risk, dangerous. And she'd never been more tempted.

She slowly nodded and stepped toward him, repressing a shiver when she clasped the crook of his arm as though her hand belonged there. She could almost feel the sparks shooting from Lexie's narrowed stare as Pascal escorted her through the crowd of high-stakes gamblers.

There was no need to ask where they were headed. The sexual heat hung like an aura between them, conveying more than any words their destination.

She saw his nostrils flare and wondered absently if he'd scented the musky bouquet at the juncture of her thighs, caught the whiff of her arousal.

Their reflections became visible as they approached the mirrored double doors of a private elevator. They truly were light and shade, fire and ice. Together they looked...perfect.

Her upswept blonde hair shone silver-bright next to the styled blue black of Pascal's. Her slender body encased in unrelenting white was sharp contrast to his powerful frame in a sleek, dark, tailored suit.

Even in stilettos she barely reached Pascal's dark-stubbled jaw and she wished, not for the first time, that she hadn't inherited her mother's petite gene. She shook her head. It was such an inane concern in comparison to the grotesque, leathery wings sprouting from her spine.

Perhaps her deformity would have been easier to bear if she'd also inherited her gargoyle father's enhanced senses and strength. Instead, she was nothing more than a human with a deformity. Only time would tell if she'd age as a human, as her mother did, or stay immortal like her father.

Security men stepped aside from their positions on either side of the elevator doors and Pascal murmured a greeting before guiding her inside.

The doors pinged shut and they shot upward. When Pascal moved to face her, she dropped his arm with a shocked gasp, only to have him clasp her chin for an infinitesimal second and look into her eyes.

She felt oddly weak-kneed, powerless to prevent his touching her. She was aware that her pulse thundered in her ears as he said huskily, "I've watched you, wanted you, ached for you, from the moment I first saw you."

For your exclusive FREE story: Her Dark Guardian, and where you can find out when my next book is available, as well as other news, cover reveals and more, sign up for my newsletter: https://madmimi.com/signups/121695/join

Check out my website – http://www.melteshco.com/

You can also friend me on Facebook at https://www.facebook.com/mel.teshco

Or my author Facebook page at https://www.facebook.com/MelTeshcoAuthor

And occasionally on Twitter at https://twitter.com/melteshco

Contact me: melteshco@yahoo.com.au

If you enjoy my books I'd be delighted if you would consider leaving a review. This will help other readers find my books ☺

The three book series, Winged & Dangerous is also available HERE[1] as a boxset.

---

1. https://www.amazon.com/dp/B00U7WJ00W

About the Author

Mel Teshco loves to write scorching hot sci-fi and contemporary stories with an occasional paranormal thrown into the mix. Not easy with seven cats, two dogs and a fat black thoroughbred vying for attention, especially when Mel's also busily stuffing around on Facebook. With only one daughter now living at home to feed two minute noodles, she still shakes her head at how she managed to write with three daughters and three stepchildren living under the same roof. Not to mention Mr. Semi-Patient (the one and same husband hoping for early retirement...he's been waiting a few years now.) Clearly anything is possible, even in the real world.

Want more Mel Teshco books?
Science Fiction:
The Virgin Hunt Games:
The Virgin Hunt Games volume 1
The Virgin Hunt Games volume 2
The Virgin Hunt Games volume 3
The Virgin Hunt Games volume 4
The Virgin Hunt Games volume 5
The Virgin Hunt Games volume 6
Dragons of Riddich:
Kadin (prequel - book 1)
Asher (book 2)
Baron (book 3)
Dahlia (book 4)
Wyatt (book 5)
Valor (book 6)
The Queen (book 7)
Alien Fugitives:
Nero (book 1)
Jasper (book 2)
Sienna (book 3)
Damaris (book 4)
Zander (book 5)
Jaire (book 6)
Epello (book 7)
Alien Hunger:
Galactic Burn (book 1)
Galactic Inferno (book 2)
Galactic Flame (book 3)
Coming soon
Galactic Blaze (book 4)
Nightmix:

Lusting the Enemy (book 1)
Abducting the Princess (book 2)
Seducing the Huntress (book 3)
Winged & Dangerous:
Stone Cold Lover (book 1)
Ice Cold Lover (book 2)
Red Hot Lover (book 3)
Winged & Dangerous Box Set (all 3 books in the series)
Dirty Sexy Space continuity with authors Shona Husk and Denise Rossetti:
Yours to Uncover (book 1)
Mine to Serve (book 6)
Ours to Share (book 8)
Awakenings series with Kylie Sheaffe
No Ordinary Gift (book 1)
Believe (book 2)
Homecoming (book 3)
Standalone longer length titles: (50k-100k)
Dimensional
Mutant Unveiled
Shadow Hunter
Existence
Standalone novellas and short stories: (15k-40K)
Identity Shift
Moon Thrall
Blood Chance
Carnal Moon
Contemporary:
Desert Kings Alliance:
The Sheikh's Runaway Bride (book 1)
The Sheikh's Captive Lover (book 2)
The Sheikh's Forbidden Wife (book 3)

The Sheikh's Secret Mistress (book 4)
The Sheikh's Defiant Princess (book 5)
The Sheikh's Fake Fiancée (book 6)
The Sheikh's Royal Widow (book 7)
The VIP Desire Agency
Lady in Red (book 1)
High Class (book 2)
Exclusive (book 3)
Liberated (book 4)
Uninhibited (book 5)
The VIP Desire Agency Boxed Set (all 5 books in the series)
Box sets with authors Christina Phillips & Cathleen Ross
Sheikhs & Billionaires
Taken by the Sheikh
Taken by the Billionaire
Taken by the Desert Sheikh
Resisting the Firefighter
Standalone longer length titles: (50k-100k)
Highest Bid
As I Am
Standalone novellas and short stories: (15k-40K)
Stripped
Clarissa
Camilla
Selena's Bodyguard (also part of the Christmas Assortment Box)\
Anthologies:
Down and Dusty: The Complete Collection
The Christmas Assortment Box
Secret Confessions: Sydney Housewives

9 798223 065708